THE BOY APPRENTICED
TO AN ENCHANTER

THE BOY
APPRENTICED
TO AN ENCHANTER

by Padraic Colum

Illustrated by Edward Leight

THE MACMILLAN COMPANY · NEW YORK
COLLIER-MACMILLAN LIMITED · LONDON

CONTENTS

1367308

The Horses
of King Manus

The Horses
of King Manus

As for the youth who had tried to steal the white horse that the King owned, he was bound hand and foot and taken into the castle of the King. There he was thrown down beside the trestles of the great table, and the hot wax from the candles that lighted the supper board dripped down upon him. And it was told to him that at the morrow's sunrise he would be slain with the sword.

Then the King called upon one to finish the story that was being told when the neigh of the white horse was heard in the stable. The story could not be finished for him, however, because the one who had been telling it was now outside, guarding the iron door of the stable with a sword in his hand. And King Manus, sitting at the supper board, could not eat nor refresh himself because there was no one at hand to finish the story for him.

And that is the way that the story of The Boy Apprenticed to an Enchanter used to begin.

But first I shall have to tell you about King Manus and his three horses.

King Manus ruled over the Western Island, and he had a castle that was neither higher nor wider than any other King's castle. But he had a stable that was more strongly built than any other King's stable. It had double walls of stone; it had oak beams; it had an iron door with four locks to it. And before this door two soldiers with drawn swords in their hands stayed night and day.

In those days, if one went before a King and asked him for a gift the King might not refuse to give what was asked of him. But King Manus was hard to come to by those with requests. For before the chamber where he sat or slept there stood a servant to take the request, and if it were one that might not be brought to him, to make an excuse for the King.

It was all because of the King's three horses—a white horse, a red horse, and a black horse. The white horse was as swift as the plunging wave of the sea, the red horse was as swift as fire in the heather, and the speed of the black horse was such that he could over-take the wind of March that was before him, and the wind of March that was behind could not overtake him.

Many had tried to get one of the King's horses by request or by robbery. But those who would ask for a gift were kept away from the King, while the stone walls, double thick, with the door of iron with four locks to it, kept robbers outside. Besides, there were the two soldiers with drawn swords in their hands to prevent the horses being taken out of the stable by any one except their own grooms. And so it was thought very certain that King Manus would never lose his famous horses.

But this very night, when the King and his lords were at supper, the neigh of a horse in the stable was heard. Then it was that the storyteller stopped in his story. The trampling of a horse was heard. Straight out King Manus ran, and his harper and his storyteller and his lords ran with him. When they came to the stable they saw that the two soldiers were sitting be-fore the iron door fast asleep, with the swords on the ground before them. And the locks were off the door of iron.

Just as they came there the iron door of the stable

opened and the King's white horse was led out. He who had the rein was a strange youth dressed in foreign dress. The youth was about to spring on the horse's back when those who were with the King sprang upon him and held him and held the bridle of the horse.

And having secured the youth they went into the stable, and they found the red horse and the black horse eating at their mangers. They led the white horse back and put him in his own stall. The watchers who had been before the stable door could not be wakened, so those who were with the King carried them to another place, and left two others, the harper and the storyteller, to keep watch, with the soldiers' swords in their hands. As for the youth who had tried to steal the white horse, he was placed as has been told you, and every one there knew what doom would befall him.

It was then that the King called upon one to finish the story that was being told him when the white horse had neighed. It was then that he sat at the supper board, not able to take rest nor refreshment on account of his not having heard the story to its end. And it was then that one of the lords said to the King, "Let the youth who is lying bound beside the trestles of the table tell us what it was that made him go into such danger to steal one of the horses of King Manus."

The King liked that saying, and he said, "Since my storyteller abides outside guarding the door of the stable, I will have this youth tell us the story of why he entered into such danger to steal one of my horses. And more than that. I declare that if he shows us that he was ever in greater danger than he is in this night I shall give him his life. But if it is not so shown the story he tells will avail him nothing, and he shall perish by the sword at the morrow's sunrise."

Then the youth was taken from where he lay by the trestles of the table, and the cords that bound him were loosened. He was put in the storyteller's place, and fresh candles were lighted and set upon the table.

"Your danger is great," said the King, "and it will be hard for you to show us that you were ever in such danger before. Begin your story. And if it is not a story of a narrow and a close escape there will be little time left for you to prepare for your death by the sword."

Thereupon the youth in foreign dress looked long into the wine cup that was handed him, and he drank a draft of the wine, and he saluted the King and the lords who sat by the King, and he said:

"Once I was in greater danger, for its mouth was close to me, and no hope whatever was given me of my saving my life. I will tell the story, and you shall judge whether my danger then was greater than is my danger now."

And thereupon the youth in foreign dress, who had tried to steal the white horse that King Manus owned, began the story which is set down here in the very words in which he told it.

PART ONE

The Story
of Eean
the Fisherman's Son

The Story of Eean
the Fisherman's Son

THE COMING OF THE ENCHANTER

My father (said the youth) was a fisherman, and he lived on this Western Island. It may be that he is still living here. His name was Anluan, and he was very poor. My own name is Eean, and the event that begins my story took place when I was twice seven years of age.

My father and I had gone down to the shore of the Western Ocean. He was fishing in the pools of the sea, and I was putting willow rods into the mouths of the fish caught so that I might carry them in my hands to the market that very day and sell them there. I looked out and saw a speck upon the water, a speck that came nearer. I kept watching it while my father dragged the pool with his net. The speck became a boat, and the boat came on without sails or oars. It was a shining boat, a boat of brass. I called to my father, and my father straightened himself up and watched it. In the boat that came toward us of its own accord there was a man standing.

The boat came into the full water between the rocks, and then it sank down, this boat of brass, until its rim touched the water. It remained still as if anchored. The man who was in the prow of the boat stepped out on the sand between my father and me.

He looked a man of high degree—like a prince or a potentate. He had a dark face and a dark, curly beard, and he had eyes that were like hawks' eyes. He had on a straight coat of a blue material covered all over with curious figures, and in his hand he held a long polished staff that had the shape of two serpents twisting together. He looked at me and I was frightened of him, and I turned to my father. But my father was standing there, holding the fishing pole in his hands, his mouth open, gasping like one of the fishes upon the rocks.

The stranger looked me over again—looked me over from my feet to my head, and then he said to my father, "There is no need that he should do aught about these fishes. I have need of an apprentice, and it would be well for you both if he should come with me."

My father then found his voice, and he said, "If my son does not sell these fishes in the market today he cannot bring back the bag of meal for our household."

Said the man from the strange boat, "Bring me to your house and I shall put down gold for every copper that your son would get in the market."

My father made a sign to me to throw the fishes back into the water. This I did, but I did it fearfully. And then my father stepped out of the pool of the sea and he made a sign to the stranger to follow us. We walked from the seashore and up the path of the cliffs, and we went through the heather of the headlands, following the goat tracks till we came to the wattled house where we lived. The man from the strange boat followed my father, and I came last of all. And when I went in and stood on the floor of our house my heart was thumping within me at the thought of what was before.

And there was the pot boiling over the fire with a few green herbs in it. There was Saba, my mother, stirring the last handful of meal among the green herbs. And there were my brothers, all older than I, sitting by the fire, waiting for the herbs and the meal to be ready.

When my mother looked toward us she saw the man from the strange boat. She thought that some crime had been committed by me or my father to bring a man of such high degree among us. She and my brothers were greatly afraid, for we were poor, and those who were high were harsh to us. But the stranger spoke softly, saying, "Good fortune has come to you from the sea today." And when they all turned toward him he said, "I who am very knowledgeable will take your son with me as an apprentice, and I shall instruct him in arts and crafts and mysteries."

My mother said, "The boy is young, sir, and we thought he would be with us for a time longer." But the man from the strange boat said, "I would not take him to instruct him in arts and crafts and mysteries if he were a day older than he is now." He said no more, but he went to the table and he laid down on it piece after piece of shining gold.

My father went to the table and held his hands around the gold. My mother looked on me who was just twice seven years old that day. I know she thought that she could never bear to part with me. But then she looked on her other sons, and she saw that they were men grown, and she thought they should have more to eat than the meal and the green herbs that were in the pot. She threw her arms around me and I knew it was a last clasp.

"He will have to go into far places to learn the arts

and crafts and mysteries that I would teach him," the stranger said.

"Will he ever come back to me?" cried my mother.

"He will come back to you when his cunning baffles my cunning," was what the stranger said.

My father took the gold that was on the table and made it into a heap. My mother took her arms from around my neck, and my brothers kissed me farewell. Then the man from the strange boat opened the door of our wattled house and went out, and I followed him.

We did not go back to the place where he had left his boat of brass. We went to another place where there was a harbor with ships. There we found a ship ready to sail for Urth.

My master sent me on board to ask the captain if he would take us on a voyage beyond Urth. The captain said that if my master would guide them past the Magnetberg he would give him the ship to sail where he would after the cargo had been landed. My master said he would do this, and we went on board the ship. It was evening now, and a breeze came up, and the ship sailed away, bringing me from the place where I was born and reared and toward the strange countries that were beyond the rim of the sea. I asked one of the sailors what was the Magnetberg, and he told me that it was a mountain of loadstone that drew the iron out of ships that came near it and left them loosened timbers upon the water.

THE INACCESSIBLE ISLAND

You have heard me so far, O King. Know now that the one to whom I was apprenticed was an Enchanter. His name is Zabulun, and in all the world there are only three Enchanters more powerful than he. The first is Chiron the Centaur, who is half man and half horse, and who taught Achilles and made him the greatest of the princes who had gone against Troy. The second is Hermes Trismegistus, the wise Egyptian. And the third is Merlin the Enchanter, whose home is in an island that is west of your Western Island.

When the night came on, Zabulun took the steering gear into his hands, and he steered the ship by a star that he alone knew. When the morning came we saw on the sea all around us the masts and the spars and the timbers of ships that had come too near the Magnetberg, and that had lost their nails and bolts, and had become loosened timbers on the waters. Those on the ship were greatly afraid, and the captain walked up and down, pulling at his beard. The night came on, and again my master took the steering gear into his own hands and steered the ship by a star that he alone knew of. And when the morning came there were no masts and spars of ships, and no loosened timbers afloat on the waters. The captain laughed and made all on the ship rejoice that they had passed the dangerous neighborhood of the Magnetberg—that mountain of loadstone that drew the iron out of ships as a magnet draws pins on a table.

We came to Urth. The great cargo that was on the ship was for the King of Urth, and it was taken off and sent over the mountain to the King's city in packs that the sailors carried on their backs. Then the captain gave the ship over to my master to sail it where he would.

He did not come upon the land nor did he look upon the country at all. But when the last pack had been carried off the ship, he said to me:

"You will have to do this, my first command to you. Go on the land. Stay by a pool that is close to the forest. Birds will come down to that pool—birds of the whiteness of swans, but smaller. Set snares and catch some of these birds, not less than four, and bring them to me uninjured."

And I went on the land and came to the pool that was close to the forest. And there I saw the birds that were of the whiteness of swans, but smaller. I watched them for a while so that I might know their ways. Then I made a crib of rods and set it to catch the birds. One went under the crib, and I pulled the string and caught the first bird. And then, hours afterward, I caught another. And waiting and watching very carefully, I caught a third. The fourth bird was wary, and I feared I should not catch it, for night was coming down and the birds were gathering to fly away. One remained near the crib, and its neck was stretched toward it. But then it shook its wings, and I thought it was going to fly to the others. It went under the crib. Then I pulled the string and caught the fourth bird.

I brought the birds to the ship, and my master gave them grains to feed on. At night we sailed away. My master held the steering gear while it was dark, but when light came he gave it to me to hold. Then he unloosed one of the birds. It flew in the middle distance, winging slowly, and remaining a long time in sight. He told me to hold the course of the ship to the flight of the bird.

At night he took the steering gear again into his hands and held the ship on her course. In the daylight he unloosed another bird and ordered me to steer by its flight. And this was done for two more days.

The morning after the last of the white birds had been freed my master bade me look out for land. I saw something low upon the water. "It is the Inaccessible Island," said my master, "where I have my dwelling and my working place." He steered the ship to where the water flowed swiftly into a great cave that was like a dragon's mouth. In that cave there was a place for the mooring of ships. The Enchanter moored the ship in its place, and then he took me up the rocky landing place.

There was a flight of great steps leading from the landing place—it was in a cave as I have told you—up to the light of day. There were a thousand wide, black steps in that flight. The Enchanter took into his hands the black staff that was shaped as two serpents twisting together, and he took me with him up the stairway.

We came out on a level place and I saw a high castle before me. There was no wall around the castle, and there was no gate to be opened. But when I came near it I found I could take no step onward. I went up, and I went down, and I tried to go onward, but I could not. Then Zabulun the Enchanter said to me:

"Around this castle of mine is a wall of air. No one can see the wall, but no one can pass it. And a bridge of air crosses my wall of air. Come now with me and I will take you over the bridge."

As the wall of air that went round the Enchanter's castle was not to be seen, neither was the bridge that went across the wall of air. But I saw my master climbing up and walking across as on a bridge. And although I saw nothing before me nor beneath me, I climbed upon something and walked across something. Following him I went downward and into the courtyard of the castle.

Within that courtyard there was a horse of brass with a giant man of brass upon it, the giant man holding a great bow in his hands. My master said to me, "If one came over the bridge of air without my authority, the arrow of that bow would be loosened, and he who came across the bridge would be slain by this giant man of brass." We went within the castle. In the hall were benches and tables, and there were statues holding torches in their hands standing by the wall. Also in that hall there was the statue of a women holding a dart in her hand. When my master came within, the statue that held the dart flung it, and the dart struck a gleaming ruby that was in the wall. Lights came into the torches that the statues held, and all the hall was lighted up.

I sat with my master at a table, and the statues

moved to us, bringing us wine and fruits. We ate and drank, and afterward a golden figure came to the Enchanter and, sitting down before him, played a game of chess with him.

The next day my master showed me more of the wonders of the Inaccessible Island. No ships came near, for there was no way to come to that island except by following the birds that were of the whiteness of a swan and that flew always in the middle distance. On this island Zabulun the Enchanter had lived for longer than the lifetimes of many men, studying magic and all the ways of enchantment. And for three years I, Eean, the son of the fisherman of the Western Island, stayed with him, learning such things as were proper for one apprenticed to an Enchanter to know.

THE ENCHANTER GOES TO BABYLON

In the three years that were passed on the Inaccessible Island, nothing that is worth my telling happened, O King. But at the end of the three years my master said to me, "We will leave the Inaccessible Island, for I have mighty business before me." And when I asked, "Where do we go, O master?" he answered, "We go to Babylon."

And then, when it was the first day after the new moon, we descended the black stairway that led into the cave where the waters came. There we found a boat of brass that was like the boat that came to the Western Island on the day when my father and I were fishing in the pools of the sea. We went into that boat of brass, and it took us through the water, steering itself. We rested on lonely islands, and at last we came to a mainland, and there the Enchanter left the boat to sink beneath the water. As travelers then we went on. We came to a town, and there my master bought for himself and me the clothing of merchants. Then we came to the river that flows toward Babylon. Men go down the river in round boats that are made of rods woven together. In every boat a live ass is carried, and when the cargo is landed the boats are broken up, for they cannot go back against the current of the river. And the cargo is loaded on the asses and brought into the market in Babylon. And whatever the merchants buy in Babylon is loaded on the asses, and the asses are driven back over the mountains into the country that these men came from.

And in such boats we went down the river and came into Babylon. No city in the world is as mighty or as wonderful as Babylon. It has three hundred and sixty-five streets, and in every street there are three hundred and sixty-five palaces, and to every palace there are three hundred and sixty-five steps leading up to its door of gold and ebony. The streets, when we came into them, were thronged with mighty, black-bearded men. I was much in dread when I stood in those great streets and looked on the mighty men who went through them.

In the center of the city were the palace and the wide-spreading gardens of the King. In those gardens, as my master told me, were one or two of all the beautiful or terrible animals of the world. Those gardens I will speak of again, O King, for it was within them that I came upon the danger that was greater than the danger that I am now in.

But first the Enchanter showed me that great wonder that was near the gardens—the Tower of Babylon. It was a red tower spiraling very high into the air. Outside of it there were steps that went round it and to the very top of it—a thousand steps. And on the top of the tower, resting against the Spear of Nimrod, was the Magic Mirror of Babylon. Zabulun the Enchanter made me look to the top, and I was made fearful by looking so high.

Oh, that I might tell you, King Manus, of the wonders of the Tower of Babylon! In the shadow of it there slept two mighty ones—the two Genii who guarded Babylon, Harut and Marut they were named. Giant beings they were. As they slept there the beard of each was spread across his mighty chest, and it was a beard so broad that no horse of the mighty horses that the King owned could leap across it. Very great but very old were Harut and Marut, the Genii who guarded Babylon.

I was made fearful by looking to the top of the tower. And then I was made still more fearful by the words that Zabulun said to me. "We have come here," he said, "to steal the Magic Mirror of the Babylonians.

"It is there on the top of the tower," said the Enchanter, "resting against the Spear of Nimrod. One looking into that mirror sees all the Kings of the world. The one who threatens Babylon is shown with a spear raised in his hand. And if a King should bring an army against Babylon, the number of its men and the ways by which it comes would be shown in the mirror. The Babylonians, by means of this Magic Mirror of theirs, are always ready for their enemies, and because of this no King in all the world will venture to make war on Babylon.

"But we shall steal the mirror and make the Tower of Babylon fall. Know that I, Zabulun, was once a

Prince of Babylon. They dishonored me, the men of Babylon, and drove me out of their city. And for that I shall make an end of their pride and an end of their security.

"Fear not. It will not be hard to steal the mirror and throw down the tower. Know that the King of the city is a foolish King, and that he cares only for his gardens and for the beautiful and terrible beasts that he can bring into them. And as for the Genii who guard Babylon—behold them! They are mighty beings, truly, Harut and Marut! Immeasurably old are they, and they pass their days in sleep beside the tower that they guard. I say to you that it will not be hard to overthrow the tower, and take away from the Babylonians the Magic Mirror that is their security."

As Zabulun spoke the terrible beasts in the King's gardens roared mightily, and Harut and Marut, the mighty beings who slept in the shadow of the Tower of Babylon, turned in their sleeping. The flocks of birds that had built nests in their beards (the oldest owl and the littlest hummingbird were among them) flew up and rested on the steps of the tower.

The black-bearded men of Babylon passed in their throngs, while he who was once a prince in their city, and who was now Zabulun the Enchanter, stood there with his staff in his hands and smiling to himself. And I, Eean, the Boy Apprenticed to the Enchanter, felt as if I were falling—falling down from the top of the tower.

THE PALACE OF THE KING OF BABYLON

AND now at the supper board of King Manus those who were eating, or drinking, or whispering to each other as the youth began his story, became silent and eager when he spoke of Babylon and the Tower of Babylon. The King himself was anxious to hear about that city that was the greatest in the world, and about the King who was the mightiest of all Kings, and he commanded the attendants to cease going here and there. So the servers and chamberlains and stewards, with the dishes, and napkins, and rods of office in their hands, stood still behind those who were seated at the table. The lords leaned forward with their eyes upon the youth who sat in the storyteller's place, and the King made a sign for him to tell on. But the youth Eean was speechless for a while. Such was the memory of the high Tower of Babylon upon him that had he been standing he would have fallen down. His head sank on the arm rest of the chair, and those near him who touched his hand felt it chilled. Then King Manus signaled for a chamberlain to go to him, and he went and wiped Eean's brow with a napkin, and then brought him a goblet of the richest wine. He raised up his head and drank, and looked down the table, and saw the high candles that burned brightly, and saw the face of the King and the faces of the lords who sat with the King. But for a while his look was the look of a man whose spirit is in another place. He heard the words that were spoken around him—words that were about the King of Babylon, and the King of Babylon's palace. The youth listened to these words and went on to speak of what befell him.

The walls of the King's palace (said Eean, the Boy Apprenticed to an Enchanter) make seven circles, one wall rising higher than the other, and each wall having a different color. The first wall is white, the second wall is black, and the third wall is scarlet; the fourth wall is blue, the fifth wall is orange, the sixth wall is plated with silver, and the seventh wall is plated with gold. I was filled with wonder when I looked on the walls of the King's palace.

The Enchanter that day had put on the dress of a merchant, but under it he had left his own garb—the straight coat that had the curious figures upon it. He took into his hand the staff that was made of two serpents twisting together, and he told me that the time had come to go to the palace and speak with the King.

At an early hour, before it was yet market time, we went through the streets of the city. The soldiers let us pass through the Gate of Brass along a way that has on each side great lions carved in stone. We came to the palace, and my master spoke to the doorkeepers and they permitted us to enter. We went through the outer courts where there were soldiers who carried naked swords in their hands. And because my master gave himself out to be a merchant from far-off parts, and because the King greatly desired to speak with those who came from far-off parts, we were brought into the presence of the King of Babylon.

He looked, O King Manus, like a King that was of a long line of Kings. His black beard was powdered with gold, and spices burned before him. But his face was white, and it was like the face of a man in a dream. Only one person stood near him—a dwarf from the Country of the Dwarfs. He had on his head a crown of scarlet feathers.

When we came before him, and after we had

bowed, the King looked upon us. He spoke to my master, and said, "What have you to sell, merchant?"

And my master, before he spoke, let fall his merchant's robe, and he showed himself in the straight garb that was covered with curious figures—the garb of a Magus it was.

"What I have to sell," he said, "is the meaning of dreams, O King."

And now, O King Manus, I have to tell of a cheat worked upon a King, and of a cheat worked by my master, Zabulun the Enchanter, upon the King of Babylon. Pretending to speak of the meaning of dreams he led the King to destruction, hoping thereby to encompass the destruction of Babylon.

The King of Babylon turned to his ancient dwarf and he said, "Remind me of my dreams." And then the ancient dwarf said to the King, "Of the three dreams that seemed remarkable to you, O King, the first was the Dream of the Three Dishes."

"It is even so," said the King. "I dreamed that there were three dishes set before me, no more than three dishes. And then I dreamed that afterward these three dishes were hidden from me and were not to be found. There was no one to tell me the signification of this dream."

"The signification of this dream," said Zabulun the

Enchanter cunningly, "is easy to discover. In the lore of the Chaldeans a dish signifies a treasure. You have dreamed of a threefold treasure that is hidden away."

But the dwarf who was beside the King spoke up and said, "Why does a dish signify a treasure?"

"That is something I may not reveal," said my master, Zabulun the Enchanter, and he turned to the dwarf the staff that was formed of two serpents twisting together. The end of the staff lifted itself as though the serpents were rising up. The dwarf covered his eyes, and cried out, "O Magus!"

"Remind me of the second dream that was considered remarkable," said the King. And the dwarf said, "The second dream was the Dream of the Laden Ass."

"It is even so," said the King. "I dreamed that I looked down the Way of the Lions, and there came along the way a laden ass. Of that dream, also, the skilled ones could tell me nothing."

"And yet the dream is plain," said the Enchanter, looking full into the eyes of the King. "A laden ass signifies a treasure found—your dream is of a treasure being brought into your palace."

"It is so," said the ancient dwarf with the crown of scarlet feathers upon his head. "In dreams an ass is always laden with treasure."

"And what was my third dream?" said the King.

"Your third dream," said the ancient dwarf, "was the Dream of the Arrows."

"It is even so," said the King of Babylon. "I dreamed of many arrows that were shot upward to a great height."

And then the King was silent, and he and the dwarf looked upon Zabulun the Enchanter. But Zabulun took a step nearer to them, and he said:

"In the lore of the Chaldeans, arrows shot upward signify a very high tower. I can tell you now the significance of your three dreams, O King. They are of a treasure that is to come into your possession. The treasure is hidden. It is hidden beneath a tower. The height to which the arrows were shot shows that the treasure is hidden under the highest of towers— under the Tower of Babylon."

At the mention of the Tower of Babylon, O King of the Western Island, a great fear came over me, for I knew that it was now that Zabulun's plan for the taking of the Magic Mirror was being put into practice. And it seemed to me that fear came over the ancient dwarf too, for he fell down upon his face. But rage grew in the King, and his black brows drew together in a frown.

"Are you one who would have the King make search for treasure beneath the Tower of Babylon?" he cried out.

"No search need be made there," said Zabulun the Enchanter. "And yet if the King should dream of treasure again it is proper that he should sacrifice a black cock upon the place where the treasure has been shown to be hidden. If that be done the dream will be banished and will come to the King no more. I speak as a Magus. But now I have shown you the meaning of the three dreams, and there is no more to be shown." And saying this the Enchanter put the garb of a merchant over the robe of the Magus. A cup was handed to him and a cup was handed to me also. This was to signify to us that our speech with the King was at an end. There was wine in our cups, but bitterness had been mixed with the wine, to signify that what had been told the King was not pleasing to him.

We went from the presence of the King, and when we were far outside the palace my master said to me:

"It will come about that the King will search for the treasure that I have put into his dreams. Moreover, he will speak to others of this treasure, and they, too, will search for it. It will come about that these many searchers, digging for the treasure, will break upon the foundations of the Tower of Babylon. Thereupon I will take the Magic Mirror and make myself the master of the Babylonians." 1367308

This he said to me as I went with him from the King's palace along the Way of the Lions. I was afraid, and it seemed to me that the lions that were in stone looked fiercely down on us as we passed.

THE KING OF BABYLON

WE lived for a whole moon in Babylon, my master Zabulun and I, before the danger that was greater than the danger that is upon me now showed itself to me. Just before the hour of the market we would go through the streets of the city and toward the great market place. Throngs of people would be there, gathered together for buying or selling, or for talk of the happenings of the day before. My master would take me to a shady place, and we would sit there, resting or refreshing ourselves with drafts of the wine of the palm.

And Zabulun would tell me that the King we had spoken with was the most foolish King who had ever ruled over Babylon. "Great and terrible he seems when he sits upon his throne in his palace," Zabulun would say, "but for all that he is foolish, and he delights more to come into the market and hear the talk of strangers than to sit in his council chamber."

Again and again Zabulun would speak of the King, and he would say: "Often he comes here, and he sits in the market place and talks with all comers, which is against the customs of the Kings of Babylon. We will see him come here, and we will watch him do what is reported of him."

Seated in the market in a shady place I would watch the throngs that moved about there. I saw the merchants who had come down the river in such round boats as we had voyaged in. They brought casks of the wine of the palm to the market. And I saw those who had come from Arabia with spices, and my master would tell me how these spices had been gathered. Some had frankincense that grows on trees that are guarded by winged serpents. Only with smoke of burning styrax could they drive the serpents from the trees. And others had cassia that is found in a shallow lake guarded by fierce, batlike creatures. To gather it men have to cover themselves all over with the hides of cattle, leaving openings for their eyes only. And there are the merchants who have the labdanum that settles on low bushes, and that sticks to the beards of he-goats that go among the bushes. Others have the cinnamon that is used by birds to build their nests against high cliffs. Men cannot climb these cliffs to gather the sticks of cinnamon, but they make the birds bring into their nests such weights as break the nests down and so strew on the ground the sticks of cinnamon. They slaughter cattle under the cliffs, and the birds fly into their nests with great pieces of the meat, and the weight of these pieces of meat breaks down the nests. And so men gather cinnamon in Arabia.

And one day my master showed me the King of Babylon as he came into the market place.

He wore a black cloak that had only one stripe of purple in it, and a boy went beside him holding an Indian hound on a leash. Having come into the market the King seated himself in a special place, and he drank wine and ate honey cakes, and talked with the strangers that were brought before him, and let himself be gaped at by throngs of people. And then, from one to another of those who were around him, my master and I heard it said, "The King, surely, has had remarkable dreams."

In three days my master was sent for by the King, and he came into the palace again bringing me with him, and he was saluted as a Magus. The King's dreams were told to him. The first dream was of a drinking cup that blazed with fire, and the second dream was of a ram-headed man with golden horns, and the third dream was of a soldier in a black cloak. All those dreams, according to those in the palace who considered dreams, were of a treasure. Zabulun, my master, agreed that assuredly they were of a treasure, knowing that whatever the King dreamed of after he had put the thought of a treasure into the minds of those in the palace would be thought to be of that and of nothing else.

Then speaking as a Magus he told them that the blazing fire of the drinking cup, the golden horns on the ram-headed man, and the blackness of the soldier's cloak all signified the Tower of Babylon. The King and the ancient dwarf became very silent when my master spoke of the tower. It was then that the Enchanter took the staff that was made of two serpents twisting together into his right hand and declared that in order to make the dream of the tower cease to trouble him, the King should sacrifice a black cock in the lowest place of the tower.

Wine was brought us then, and my master and I drank, and this time no bitterness had been put into the wine. We were given permission to go, and we went from the palace.

As for the King and the ancient dwarf who was with him, they took horses and they rode to the Tower of Babylon, the dwarf bringing with him a black cock for the sacrifice. Harut and Marut, the sleeping guardians of Babylon, looked on, but they went past them and within the tower. In the lowest place in the tower they made preparations for the sacrifice of the black cock.

Zabulun and I sat in the market place and waited, for my master said to me, "That which happens to the King, no matter how great it may be, he will speak of it in the market. We shall wait here and see if the King will come here on his way back from the tower."

So in the market place we sat, my master and I. And in the tower the King and the ancient dwarf took the black cock and fastened him by a leg to a ring that was in a very light board in the floor. The cock, fluttering upward, lifted the board. Looking down, they saw a chamber beneath. They went down into that chamber, the King and the ancient dwarf, and behold! they found in it a treasure of silver pieces, each piece marked with the mark of a King of the old times in Babylon.

Soon Zabulun, seated in the shade in the market place, showed me the King and the ancient dwarf as they came among the throng. The King seated himself in his special place and drank wine and ate cakes of honey. My master, watching him from afar, knew that he talked about the treasure he had found, for the dwarf who went with him opened a leather bag and showed certain pieces that made those around them gape in wonder.

Not long were the King and the ancient dwarf there before the Hour of the Market came to its close. Those in the market left and went to their homes. My master and I likewise departed. But those who had listened to the King brought with them the memory of the wonder they had been told about. A treasure was hidden beneath the tower—that was the thought that now possessed every one. And when dusk had fallen upon the city, companies of men made their way toward the tower, carrying with them spades and picks. The next day, when the King came with the ancient dwarf, he found that all around the tower, and all around the place where Harut and Marut slept, trenches and holes had been dug.

He himself, with a company of men, went down

into the lower chamber where the treasure of silver pieces had been found, and there they began to delve. The King found no treasure that day.

When he came out of the lower chamber he found many around the tower digging and delving. He forbade them to do this, and he set guards around the tower. But in the night those who were set to guard the tower began to delve.

The digging and delving within and around the tower went on in secret as well as openly. My master took me to show me what was being done. "Foolish is the King, and foolish are the people of Babylon," he said. "What I have told you will befall them. Very soon they will strike at the foundations of the tower, and the tower will stand no more. Then will I take to myself the Magic Mirror and make myself the master of the Babylonians."

THE GENII WHO GUARDED BABYLON

O KING of the Western Island (said Eean, the Boy Apprenticed to an Enchanter), I was there in Babylon for the whole of a moon before the danger that was greater than my present danger overtook me.

Often Zabulun, my master, went to the palace of the King, bringing me with him. And the King would now receive us in his cool chamber, and he would permit my master to seat himself on a purple cushion in his presence. The King would ask him about the ways of governing a kingdom, or he would tell him of his wonderful gardens, and of the strange and terrible beasts he had there. Or else he would talk about a mighty treasure that was to be found, and of the beasts he would buy for his gardens when that treasure came into his hands. Zabulun would tell the King of beasts he had seen or heard of—of the aurochs with its mighty horns, of the unicorn that was so white and so swift, of the satyr that is so marvelous that no one knew whether it was a wonderful beast or a wild man. And often, as they sat there talking, the King would have his servants stir up the beasts in his gardens so that their roarings might be heard by those in the palace.

Over the King and the King's ancient dwarf there had come a change, I thought. For the dwarf with the crown of scarlet feathers on his head would stand silent before the throne, silent even though the King spoke to him, silent as if listening to the sound that the spades and picks made on the ground around the

Tower of Babylon. And the King no longer had the look of a ruler on his face, but had the look of a watcher and a waiter. There had come a change over my master also. Zabulun the Enchanter had eyes like yellow lamps, and they had become wider and more gleaming as the digging and delving around the Tower of Babylon went on. I could hardly see his face. And I began to have a great fear of Zabulun, even though he was kind to me, and had taught me many things.

And now I come to the day when that danger beset me that was greater than my present danger. That morning I had walked in the King's gardens with Zabulun, my master. I saw the great palm trees that grew there. So high and so shapely they grew that I was made to think again of the Tower of Babylon, and I was shaken by my thought. I looked along the great avenue of palms, and I saw down to the lake where the King's blue herons flew. And from the lake coming toward us I saw a young girl. She had laid the long blue feathers of the heron across her breast, and I saw her white forehead and her white knees, for her dress was the dress of a woman of the mountains. But she, seeing Zabulun and me, sprang as a young deer springs, and went among the palm trees. I kept thinking of that girl, and how free she was, and how no terror of a falling tower beset her as she went by the lake where the King's blue herons flew or rested.

Again Zabulun, my master, sat in the King's presence, and the ancient dwarf and I attended on them. The dwarf's head hung down where he stood, and he muttered. The King's voice was low when he spoke, but Zabulun spoke loudly. Also his yellow eyes shone as he twisted around his finger a purple strip that had been torn off the King's robe.

And suddenly there came the mighty roaring of beasts in the King's gardens. The dwarf looked at the King, and the King spoke to the dwarf, and there was astonishment on both their countenances, for no command had been given to have the beasts stirred up. The King rose from where he sat and went to the doorway. I, too, saw what he saw. The doorkeepers, and even the soldiers who had naked swords in their hands, were fleeing as before some terror. The King shouted his commands, but no one heeded them. I looked upon the King, and the King's wrath was terrible to behold.

And then I saw the King himself draw back in fear. What was it that approached? I, too, looked, and there, O King Manus, as I declare to you, I saw

Harut and Marut, the giant guardians of Babylon, come through the outer courts and toward the chamber where the King stood.

They were naked but for their great beards and their flowing hair. They came with great strides, but their heads and their hands were swaying about like the heads and hands of men suddenly waked out of a deep slumber. The ancient dwarf saw them approach, and he screamed out and fled.

The King went out of the chamber and into the hall where the great pillars were. I called to my master, and he arose from the cushions where he sat, and he looked upon the two who came nearer. Along the line of the pillars Harut and Marut came, but Zabulun the Enchanter looked upon them without fear.

The King fell upon his knees as they came near him. My master's face did not become fearful, but he, too, went down on his knees as if powerful and unseen hands had forced him down. His eyes did not lose their look of scorn, but he knelt even as the King knelt. The King and the Enchanter were both Princes of Babylon, and when Harut and Marut showed themselves in their might, there was something within them that forced them to sink down on their knees.

And nearer and nearer Harut and Marut came,

their heads swaying about and their arms hanging down. Nearer and nearer they drew. They touched the head of the King, and the King lay prone on the ground as though the life had left him. They came to where Zabulun the Enchanter knelt. But not on Zabulun's head did they lay their hands. They took him by the arms and they held him. Turning around, they dragged him along the line of the pillars. I saw him being drawn across the outer court and through one of the great doorways of the King's palace.

And then it seemed that I was the only one left in the palace of the Kings of Babylon. The King did not stir where he lay prone, and the dwarf did not return, and the doorkeepers did not show themselves any more. I ran from the chamber, and out through one of the great doors, and into a place where branches of trees seemed to shield me from the terror that had fallen upon the palace. And I did not know then that I was running from terror clear into the mouth of danger.

Dreadful things had happened outside as well as within the palace of the King. The beasts that were in the gardens had broken out of their pits and their cages. I saw the beasts and I felt them all around me. I saw the hippopotami as they lay with their backs against the crimson wall of the palace. I saw the zebras stamp between the yellow wall and the blue wall, and ostriches run between the black and the white walls. And when I looked back from where I was in the gardens I saw monkeys climb on the golden and silver walls, frightened by the lions that went roaring through the courts of the palace. I ran on and on, down the great avenue of palms and toward the lake where the King's blue herons flew or rested.

I ran on. But I had gone aside from the avenue of the palms, seeing a great buffalo that stood in my way. Something caught at my feet as I ran on the clear ground, and being tripped, I fell into a deep pit. I lay there, and I looked to the sky, and I saw that the pit narrowed to the top, and for that reason was hard to climb out of. It was higher again by my own height, as I saw when I stood up thinking of a way that might get me out.

But then there came a sound that made me look downward, a hissing sound. And when I looked down I saw into what place I had fallen—into the Pit of the Serpent. In the shadow of the pit there was a dreadful snake. It was still in its coils, but its head was raised, and it was swaying toward me.

Then, O King of the Western Island, I was in a

danger greater than I am in now. This snake was mighty enough to crush a man, and from that pit there was no escape without help, and at that moment there was no help. The snake raised itself higher, and its eyes fastened my eyes. Judge, then, of my danger, and whether it was not greater than the danger I am in now as I sit here with the gleam of the slaying sword before my eyes.

And then I heard a whisper that seemed to come to me from the sky. I drew my eyes from the snake's eyes and I looked to the top of the pit. Bending from the opening was a girl, and she had in her hands a little drum. She began to beat on the drum, and the snake's head that was swaying toward me began to sway sideways. The girl beat again on the drum, and the snake's head swayed and swayed and went down upon its coils. At last the dreadful head was at rest, and the eyes of the snake no longer fastened themselves upon my eyes.

The girl who stood above the pit put down a board for me to climb up by. I climbed, and I stood outside the pit, and I looked upon the girl, and I saw the blue heron's feathers laid across her breast. Then I sank down on the ground, and for a while I knew no more of the world's happenings.

AGAIN THE HORSES OF KING MANUS

It was as if the eyes of the snake were still upon him. Eean stopped in his story, and his eyes were wide as if they looked upon a terrible thing. One of the servers brought him a cup of wine and placed it in his hands, but although he kept his fingers around it, he did not raise it to his lips.

Nor did he appear to hear what was being said around the King's supper table: "A great danger the boy was in, truly." "The danger he is in now is not as great as the danger he has told us of." "We must hear the end of this story." "It seems that he is too fearful to tell us any more." This last speech came to the ears of King Manus. "Be not so fearful, boy," said the King. "You have been in a greater danger than ever I heard a man speak of, and by my sword, you are in less danger now than you were then. Drink the wine that is in it and keep the cup you have for a remembrance. I would have you at your ease, too, for we will sit here and listen to the rest of your story."

When the King said this the lords who were sitting around the supper board applauded, and then the stewards signaled to the attendants to bring more lights in. Fresh candles were put upon the board, and fresh torches were put into the sconces, and fresh logs were put upon the hearth. When all this was done the King and his lords turned their faces to Eean, for they were ready to listen to the rest of the story. But the boy had not seated himself in the storyteller's chair: still he was standing with the winecup between his hands, and still his eyes were widened as if a terrible thing was before him.

It was then, as they were waiting for him to begin, that the neigh of a horse was heard again. It was a very shrill neigh, and every one in the supper hall was startled by it. Out they rushed, King and lords, stewards, servers, and attendants, and they neither stopped nor stayed until they came before the King's great stable. Then they could hardly believe what their eyes looked upon: the iron door of the stable was open wide; the watchers were there, but their heads were bent in sleep and their swords were upon the ground. Through the open door of the stable came the whinnyings and the plungings and the tramplings of a horse. Quickly they went into the stable. There, by the light of the torches that the attendants held, they saw the white horse and the red horse still in their stalls, but the black horse they saw rearing above a figure that was prone upon the ground.

The blaze of their torches made the black horse swerve so that his hoofs did not come down upon the figure that was upon the stable floor. The horse was taken hold of and put back into his stall. Then the attendants raised up the one who was upon the ground. "Another one come to steal my horses," cried King Manus. "Well, this one shall pay the penalty that the other has been delivered from."

They took up the one who was on the floor of the stable. They locked the stable door again and they put a double watch before it. They brought the one whom they had taken into the supper hall; a lad, younger even than Eean, this second robber seemed.

Eean was standing by the storyteller's seat as they came into the supper hall. Looking upon the one they brought in he cried out in the voice of the heart-broken, "O Bird-of-Gold, why didst thou peril thyself by staying here? Too faithful to me thou hast been!" Hearing this speech, all looked on the one who was called Bird-of-Gold: it was then that they saw they had taken, not a youth as they had supposed, but a young girl whose dress was a youth's dress.

In the light of the torches and candles they looked

at her wonderingly. She had knitted brows and heavy eyelids that gave to her face the look of one who ponders deeply. And there was such fire behind the depths of her eyes that it seemed as if her thought was always burning. But her lips were colorless and her cheeks were thin and sunken; her hair and her eyes and her eyebrows were dead black. And when they went to bind her as they had bound Eean they saw that her hands were finely shaped and yet strong and hard.

"Who is she?" said King Manus.

"I have told you of her," said Eean. "This is she who found me in the Pit of the Serpent and who drew me away from the venom of the snake."

There was silence for a while, and then the King said, "The chance that was given you shall be given her also. If she can show us that she was in a danger greater than the danger she is in now her life shall not be taken. If she cannot show that, she shall be slain by the sword on tomorrow's sunrise."

At that some of the trouble that was on Eean's face seemed to leave it. He cried out, "O Bird-of-Gold, tell the King the story of your adventures from the beginning. Think thee, Bird-of-Gold, of the terrible things you have gone through and speak to the King and the lords of them. This King is very generous, and you may win your life from him."

The girl who was called Bird-of-Gold turned to the King her face that seemed to him to be like the face of a slave and a victorious warrior. Her hands were bound before her and her black hair fell over her breast. Like one who was ever ready in deed and word, as soon as King Manus made a gesture, she began.

PART TWO

*The Story of
Bird-of-Gold who
was the Bramble
Gatherer's Daughter*

The Story of Bird-of-Gold who was the Bramble Gatherer's Daughter

HOW THE BRAMBLE GATHERER'S DAUGHTER WENT TOWARD HER FORTUNE

I AM called Bird-of-Gold (said the girl, beginning her story), but that name did not belong to me until I was a girl grown. Before that I had no name. In the city where I was born and where I lived I was known as "the bramble gatherer's child."

My father was the poorest of all the men of that town. He gathered brambles and thorns in the wilderness and brought them in a bundle to the hut where we lived. Then, while he was gathering another bundle on another day, I would go through the town selling the brambles and thorns for stuff for the people's fires. My mother I never knew. I grew up with my father, and we two had even less than the sparrows. I had no playmate and no friend, and what I got for the thorns and brambles I sold brought us but little to eat.

One day as I passed along the street of the city it came into my mind that I was grown to be a girl. The thought that I should go from the city grew in me from that time. My father would miss me, but he would flourish better if there were one, and not two, to eat the scanty meal that the price of the brambles and thorns gained for us.

I got for myself the cap and jacket of a boy. Then one morning when my father had gone from the hut and had turned his face to the wilderness and his back to the city, I went out of the door and turned to the wilderness also. I took a direction that would bring me far from where my father had gone. I had dressed myself as a boy, and my thought was that I would come upon a merchant who would let me do service for him, and who, perhaps, would take me on a voyage. And I thought that I might win some fortune for myself, and that then I could return and take my father out of toil and hardship.

I came to the wilderness and I went through it. When the sun was halfway in the heavens I came to where there was a road. There was a pillar before me and that pillar had writing upon it. I read what was written there. The words were: *They who take the road to the right will come to their fortune at last, and they who take the road to the left will be ever as they have been.* When I read that writing I took the road that was to my right.

I went along that road thinking every minute that I should come upon something that would bring me to my fortune. The light faded as I went along, and soon I had to look about for some tree or cave that would give me a shelter for the night. At last I saw a hut and I went toward it. When I came before the broken door I knew the place I had been brought to. It was my father's hut—the hut I had left that morning. And as I stood before it I saw my father coming from the other side with the bundle of brambles and thorns upon his back. Then I said to myself, "How lying was the writing that said that they who took the road to their right would come at last to their fortune."

I went into the hut with my father. In the darkness he did not see that I had on the cap and jacket of a boy. He laid the bundle of brambles and thorns down on the floor while I went to prepare the meal for both of us. And while my father was lighting a fire I took off the cap and jacket of a boy and I put on my girl's dress.

My father, when he had eaten his meal, said to me, "Today when I had gathered the brambles and had made them into a bundle I lay with my head on the bundle and went to sleep. I awakened feeling some warmth near where my head lay. I looked to see if perchance the brambles and thorns had caught on fire, and, lo! what I saw laid on the bundle was the egg of a bird. The egg was still warm, and the bird that laid it must have flown as I awakened."

My father showed me the egg. It was strangely marked and was heavy for its size. I looked at it, and my father said, "Take it to the merchant tomorrow, and maybe he will give a coin for it, for surely it is remarkable."

The next day, when my father had gone into the wilderness, I went to the shop of the merchant. I showed him the egg that had the strange markings upon it, and I asked him if he would give me something for it. And when the merchant had taken the egg in his hand he said, "This is something to be shown the King. It is undoubtedly the egg of the Bird of Gold."

I was greatly stirred when I heard the merchant say this, and I thought that perhaps my fortune would come to me through this egg. I went back to the hut, and in the morning, before my father started off for his bramble gathering, two officers came and they took my father and me to the palace and before the King. And the King said, "It is known that of all creatures in the world the Bird of Gold is best worth possessing. For her claws can be made into an amulet that will bring wealth to the one who wears it, and the one who eats her heart can never be slain by his enemy. I would have the Bird of Gold whose egg you have found. You know where she lives. Catch her and bring her to me, and I shall reward you."

So spoke the King of our little country. My father and I went into the wilderness to search for the Bird of Gold around the place where the egg had been laid. And in the very place where he had lain my father put down his bundle of brambles and thorns. Laying his head upon the bundle, he went to sleep.

I watched beside the brambles and thorns. And after a time a bird came running along the ground, and went fluttering up on the bundle and made a nest for herself. Small she was, and all golden except for the blue that was under her throat, and the blue that was upon her feet. As she was making a nest for herself I put my hands upon her and caught her. I held her to my breast to keep her from fluttering away.

And I said aloud, "O bird, now I shall be rewarded for taking thee. For the King would make an amulet

of thy feet that he may have wealth, and he would eat thy heart that his enemies may not be able to slay him. Greatly will he reward me for having taken thee, O Bird of Gold."

And as I spoke to her and held her to my breast the bird made a cry that sounded as "Alas, Alas!" I looked upon her again, and my heart was filled with sorrow for the bird I had taken. Why should her claws be made into an amulet for the King, and why should her heart be eaten by him? I sat there thinking while my father slept, holding the bird very gently to my breast. And when she cried again "Alas, Alas!" I opened my hands and I let her fly away. She fluttered near for a while as if to show herself to me, and then she rose up and flew away.

My father awakened, and he said, "It is near dark, and the Bird of Gold will not come now. Perhaps we will find her on another day. The King should reward us for our search, and now we will go to him and tell him of it."

So we rose up and we went into the city. And when we came before him, my father spoke to the King and told him that the Bird of Gold was not to be seen in the places where we had searched. Then the King would have sent us away without doing any evil to us only one who was near him cried out: "Behold, O King, and decree a punishment for these two deceivers. One has declared that the Bird of Gold did not come near where they searched. But look on the dress of the girl. All around her breast are the feathers of the Bird of Gold."

Thereupon I looked down and I saw that the bird's golden feathers were all strewn around the place where I had held her to me. I was grasped by the hands and brought before the King. And he cried out, "Have you the bird hidden?" I said: "No, O King. I let the bird fly out of my hands." Then the King spoke to one who stood beside him, and he commanded that I should be taken and put upon a ship and thrown into the depths of the sea.

I was taken from my father, who wept and cried after me, and I was brought down to the river and put upon a ship. The one who was commanded by the King to take me and throw me into the depths of the sea was a man with a great hooked nose and a purple beard. On his hand was a ring with a great emerald in it. He was the captain of the King's ships.

I was put upon the ship, and the next day we sailed down the river and came out on the sea. Now, although the King had commanded that I be thrown

into the depths of the sea, I was not then in as great a
danger as I am in now, O King of the Western Island.
For the captain of his ships hated all the words that the
King gave him, and those whom the King would slay
he would save, and those whom the King would save
he would have slain. When we came into the open sea,
so that he might obey the King's word and at the same
time make a mock of it, he had me thrown into the
water, but with a rope around my waist. After I had
been plunged into the water he had me drawn out of
it, and I was left living on the ship. And from the captain who had had me plunged into the sea in such
ways and from the sailors on the ship I got the name
by which I have been known ever since—Bird-of-
Gold.

THE MAN WHO WAS HIGH
IN FORTUNE

WE landed in a country (said Bird-of-Gold,
continuing her story) that was three days' voyage
from the river's mouth. Then the sailors put swords
into their belts and marched toward a mountain that
was half a day's journey from the coast. They pitched

black tents and they built a citadel, and they made themselves into a band of robbers. He who had been the captain of the King's ships was the chief of this band.

Every day they went off to rob caravans and to make war upon the men who guarded the caravans. And always they came back, my master and his forty robbers, with no man of their band slain and with no man wounded. Very rich and powerful did they grow with the plunder they took from the caravans, and my master, the man with the hooked nose and the purple beard, grew to be a King almost. Men far and near sent him presents and men came to him promising obedience, and he had state such as had the King of my country. But he kept no men with him except his forty robbers.

Every one said of my master, the captain of the band, that nothing could come to him except good fortune, so great and so prosperous did he grow. Men marveled that so many good things came to him and so many evil things were staved off from him. And all his band swore by his good fortune. But one day a wise King who liked him greatly sent my master a message that said: "I rejoice in your good fortune, friend, but am also troubled by it. He who is so lucky must pay a great price sooner or later for his luck. Pay the price now, before it is exacted from you, and remain great and prosperous. Let the price you pay be that possession that is dearest to you."

My master, having received this message, paid heed to what was said in it, for the King who sent it was renowned for his wisdom. He made up his mind to sacrifice the possession that was dearest to him so that he might remain great and prosperous. And the possession that he considered dearest was the ring that he wore with the great emerald in it. He went down to the seacoast, taking me with him, for he would let none of the forty men know what he was about to do, and he took a boat and he went, I being with him, over the depths of the sea. Then he drew from off his finger the ring that had the great emerald in it, and he let it drop down into the depths of the sea. Afterward he sent a message back to the King, his friend, saying that he had paid the price before it was exacted of him, and that his prosperity now would never fail, and that men would ever swear by his good fortune.

After that he and his forty men went forth and won more plunder than ever they had won before. Also more men came from far and near, bringing him presents and promising him obedience.

And now, being so prosperous and so feared, my master planned to attack a city and make himself the master of the King's treasure. He told his plan to his forty men and they rejoiced one and all, and they talked to each other as if that treasure was already in their hands. I prepared the meal that was to be given him before he collected his men for the march.

The meal was of fish. The fisherman who had just come from the sea laid his net before me and I took out of it an exceedingly large and beautiful fish. I divided the fish and began to make it clean. I found within the fish something it had swallowed. It was a ring. And when I cleaned the ring I found that it was of gold and that in it was a most precious stone—a stone of emerald.

I cooked the fish and brought it to my master. And to make him rejoice I brought at the same time the ring to him. I told him that for the ring he had dropped into the depths of the sea another ring had come back to him, and that this was on account of the great good fortune that was ever with him.

He took the ring from me and he looked it all over. He cried out that this was not another ring but the same ring, and that the characters of his name were engraved upon it. And he said that it was by no means on account of his good fortune that this ring had come back to him. Thereupon he rose up and went outside, and gave command to his band that they were to disarm themselves and tie up their horses, and hold themselves back from making any attack that day. He then went into his tent and sat at the darkest part of it, his purple beard touching the ground, and all the while lamenting that his dearest possession had come back to him out of the depths of the sea.

The forty men disarmed themselves and tied up their horses and sat in little bands playing games together. I would have stayed about the encampment making bread for the band, but as I came near the tent where the kneading board was I heard a bird's cry.

I looked, and I saw near the wellhead the Bird of Gold. The bird fluttered and flew as if she wanted me to watch her. I followed where she went and I was led far from the encampment. At the edge of the wilderness she went among low bushes, and after that I could not see her any more.

Because I had seen the Bird of Gold once more I went back toward the encampment thinking about the days when I had lived in the hut of my father, the bramble gatherer, and about the day when I had left that hut, and had gone across the wilderness, and had seen the pillar on which was written that if I followed the road to the right I should come to my fortune, and about how I had come, not to my fortune, but back to the hut I had left; and I went on, thinking of how I had first heard of the Bird of Gold, and of how I had given her liberty when I might have held her for the great reward the King would have given. I went toward the encampment thinking these thoughts about myself, and thinking, too, of my master who had such fortune that men swore by the goodness of it.

I made my way toward the tent where the kneading board was. And then I saw tents overturned and lying upon the ground. I saw the horses of the band straying over the plain. And when I looked to the citadel I saw it smoking with a fire that was burning it.

There was no stir in all the encampment. I knew then that an army had come and had attacked my master and his forty men in the time that I was following the Bird of Gold or coming back from the place where she had led me. I went among the tents and I saw that the men had been killed. And I saw the purple beard of my master, cut off by some insolent enemy and left lying upon the ground.

Then I ran over the trampled grass and made for the wilderness. And when I came into the wilderness

I hid myself among the bushes that the Bird of Gold had flown into. I thought that a great army was pursuing me, and in truth I was very fearful.

HOW BIRD-OF-GOLD CAME TO HER FORTUNE

I HID at the near side of the wilderness (said the girl, Bird-of-Gold), for I was too fearful to go back to the encampment and too fearful to go farther on. I ate the wild fruits that grew on the bushes, and at night I covered myself with dried leaves and branches and slept in a hole. I thought how he had been destroyed, that man whose good fortune had been above everyone else's good fortune, and I did not know how such a one as I could keep alive. I was fearful while I slept, and when I awoke and sat upon a heap of leaves in that empty wilderness I was most miserable. I remembered the writing on the pillar that told me to take the road to the right on the day I left my father's hut and I put a curse upon the road I took. I cursed it because it had brought me, not to my fortune as the writing said it would bring me, but back to the hut I had left. And things were even worse with me from that time than they were before, for my return had brought me to the encounter with the King, and to the voyage with the captain of the King's ships, and to the dangerous place where I was now.

But then I began to think that although that road had brought me to my father's hut it had not brought me back to a life that was as it had been before. What had happened after I had come back to the hut had brought me farther away than that road could have led to. Perhaps the writing on the pillar was not lying, after all. It had said: They who take the road to the right will come at last to their fortune. Perhaps my fortune was farther away than I had thought.

Then I said to myself that my journeys were not yet ended, and that if I went on I should yet come to what the writing on the pillar had promised. I sat still for a while with this thought in my mind, and then I rose up and went through the wilderness, going straight on toward a star that was still in the sky.

I left the wilderness with its low shrubs at last, and I came out on a wide, green plain. Before going on that plain I ate again of the wild fruit that was on the bushes and I brought some of the wild fruit with me. I went on and on over the miles of grass. When it was midday I saw a whiteness upon the plain before me.

I went toward that whiteness and in a while I saw that it was all in movement. There were white living creatures there. I went on, and I came near to where there was a hollow in the plain, and I saw in that hollow a mighty flock of ducks. They were tame, for they did not rise up and fly as I came near.

I looked upon them with great astonishment. I had never seen so many ducks together. I looked them all over and I made a guess that there were a thousand ducks there. And I had never seen such beauty in ducks before. For these ducks were of a gleaming whiteness, and moreover they had a shapeliness that I had never seen in such creatures before. I thought and thought, but I could not think how they had come into this unpeopled plain in such a vast flock.

I sat down on the grass and I watched them feeding, thinking surely that some one would come and drive the flock to some market or to some great farm. I watched, and the ducks ate and ate in the hollow where they stayed. When the darkness came the thousand ducks put their heads under their wings and settled down on the ground. I pulled grass to make a bed for myself, and ate the fruit I had brought with me, and lay down in a cold place near the hollow.

I was awakened by the thousand ducks quacking

loudly, and I looked and saw that they had spread themselves over the plain and were moving in a direction. I thought I should follow the ducks, and I did, and I was able to chase away two or three foxes that would have hunted them.

They were beautiful, these thousand ducks, as they went over the green plain. They were shapely and active, and they had a wonderful soft whiteness. The drakes were not colored differently, but they had crests and tails that curled. When they knew I was with them they did not go straying here and there, but kept themselves together as a flock and went marching in a direction. I thought that they might bring me to my fortune. And then I thought that this great flock of ducks, so strangely without an owner, was my fortune.

I was faint and hungry, but I went on rejoicing in the beauty of the ducks. I gave them time to feed, and they fed. At last I came to the gate of a town. The watcher was astonished at the greatness of the flock and he called to the townspeople to come out and fill their eyes with the spectacle. They came and asked me, "Who are you, O girl?" and I made answer, "I am the girl whose fortune is in ducks." The people came on the walls of the town and looked over them,

while the ducks spread themselves out and stood still. And more and more the people marveled at the number and the extraordinary beauty of the ducks.

The people set a place apart for the ducks and they gave me a shelter in which I might rest and refresh myself. After a while I heard them say, "The officers of the great King of Babylon should see this girl and her ducks. There is a marvel here for the great King to hear about." People came to see the ducks as a spectacle, and one would say to the other, "No prince by any river in China has such a wonderful collection of ducks."

And then I was told that the officers of the great King of Babylon would come to look on my flock. These officers had come into the country to get for the King's gardens birds and beasts that were remarkable.

They came and looked on the flock and marveled that, whether they rested or were feeding, the thousand ducks harkened to my call and went as I bade them go. They spoke, admiring their shape and whiteness. And then a dwarf who had a crown of scarlet feathers on his head came among them, and the officers spoke to him. This dwarf told me they would take the flock for the King, and that they would take me also to the great city, where I would have the office of minding the ducks in the King's gardens.

So I brought the thousand ducks down to a great barge that was on the river, and I went on the barge, and the officers of the King with the dwarf that had the crown of scarlet feathers on his head went aboard it, and we sailed down the river, and we came into the great city. For two days the King had me show the wondrous flock in the market place as a spectacle for the people. All Babylon came and admired the number and the comeliness of the ducks. Afterward they were brought to the lake that was in the King's gardens. As time went on many of the flock were taken by the purveyors and killed and eaten in the palace. But still they remained a wonder for their number and their comeliness. The King often came down to look on the thousand ducks swimming on the water or staying in their companies around the lake.

BIRD-OF-GOLD IN THE KING'S GARDENS

No place in the whole world is more beautiful than the King's gardens in Babylon (Bird-of-Gold said). My white ducks, when they swam upon the lake, went among water lilies that were silver-white or all golden. Beside the lake the irises grew, depths and depths of blue and gold and cloud-colored irises. I should never have left the side of that lake if I had not wanted to be among the trees that grew in the gardens above—palm trees of many kinds, and great cedar trees in the dark branches of which the doves built their nests. Greatly did I admire the trees in the King's gardens, for I had come from a country where there were no trees. All the palms were there—the date palm, and the royal palm, and the palm of the desert. They stood nobly by themselves or they made solemn avenues that led to monuments of the Kings of Babylon. In the grass there were golden poppies and little roses that just lifted themselves above the ground. There were great monuments, too—statues of Kings and lions and chariots, and these reminded people of terrors and magnificences, and they were as a great wind that blew through the gardens.

And there were tulips on the ground, and there were golden fruits among gleaming leaves, and red pomegranates on the high trees, and there were spice trees that filled with fragrance the garments of those who passed. And all in a garden to themselves were the roses—a thousand rose trees, each tree with a thousand opened flowers. I wept when I saw that garden of roses, and I do not know why I wept.

All the birds that were lovely to look at or charming to hear singing were in that garden. The black birds with golden wings from my own country were there, and the birds of paradise from the Land of the Burning Mountain. And it was told that the nightingales of Persia and Babylon and Arabia brought their young here that they might learn to sing the more perfectly. Also there were mockingbirds that mocked every bird's song but the song of the nightingale.

As for the beasts in the King's gardens, the first one I made friends with was a lynx. He was not in a cage, but went roaming about, watching everything with eyes that never winked. And after I had come to know him and had made friends with him, the lynx brought me to the cages and the pits of the other beasts and with them I made friends.

Of all the creatures that were there the one I was most fearful of was the queen serpent that was in the Pit of the Serpent. But the serpent attracted me, and I used to sit above the pit, the lynx beside me, and watch her as she uncoiled herself and swayed her head about. And as I watched her I would beat on a little drum that I carried with me. I began to see that as I beat the drum and made music for her, the serpent would cease to sway her head and she would lower it, and then she would rest upon her coils as if she were sleeping. So I grew to have power over the serpent, and many times when I saw her try to draw down a bird that had come to the edge of the pit, I would beat upon the drum until her head sank down. Then the bird would rouse itself out of the spell that the serpent's eyes had put on it and fly away.

So I stayed in the King's gardens, part of the day with the thousand ducks that were about the lake, and part of the day with the ever-watchful lynx that went here and went there.

One day I came up from the lake after having decked myself with the blue herons' feathers that lay about. I saw two persons where none but the King or the King's ancient dwarf ever came. One was a man who wore a straight garment that had curious figures woven upon it, and who carried in his hand a staff that was formed of two serpents twisting together. The one who was with him was a boy, and my heart went out to him because he was young, and I had seen no one who was young in all my days in Babylon. The two walked in the gardens, and I ran and hid from them.

A day came soon after when I came up from the lake and did not find the lynx who was my friend. I went searching for him, and at last I came upon him. He had gone up into one of the great chariots that were for a monument to a King. I saw him watching from the chariot. I went beside him, and the lynx did not move, but kept watching, watching.

Before I saw what was coming I heard a great trampling noise. I saw trees break and fall down. Flocks of birds came flying toward me, and I saw the deer start up and run. Then I saw enormous shapes coming striding through the gardens. They were as men, but men as high as towers. As they came on, trees fell down before them, and beasts broke out of their pits and cages and crouched before them. The beasts were filled with fear, and they roared and screeched and trumpeted as if fearful things were about to happen to them. The giant men passed where I stood in the great chariot and they came to the gateway that led into the courts of the King's palace. They put their hands to the stones above the gateway, and the heavy, mortared stones fell, leaving a space high enough for the men to pass through. I looked from the King's palace toward the city, and I saw the Way of the Lions and it was black with people that fled from the palace—soldiers and servants and attendants. I saw the beasts of the gardens bound or crash through the broken gateway, entering the courts of the palace.

I saw the giant men come forth from the palace. Now they held a man by the arms and dragged him along. They crossed the gardens dragging the man, and for a time I watched the dust that their progress made.

As I watched I saw someone come fleeing from the palace. He ran on, coming straight to the place from where I watched. He stumbled as he ran, and I saw him fall into the Pit of the Serpent. It had seemed to me as I watched him that this was the boy who had walked with the strange man in the gardens.

In my hands I had the little drum whose sound

could put a spell upon the queen serpent. I ran toward the pit holding the drum. And when I bent over I saw that the head of the serpent was very near to the boy. I beat upon the drum, and the serpent heard, and her head ceased to sway about. Then her head went down, and she remained in her coils upon the ground.

I drew the boy up, and I led him to the lake and I bathed his face and his hands. The day had almost passed before he was able to speak to me. Then he told me who he was, and what the events were that had happened in the King's palace. And that boy is the one who is before you now, O King of the Western Island—Eean, the fisherman's son, who was apprenticed to the Enchanter.

HOW BIRD-OF-GOLD WENT TO THE TOP OF THE TOWER

LONG did it take Eean to tell me the whole of the story, and when he had told it and I had gathered and put together all of it, I said to him, "Not yet has the tower fallen, and ere it comes down one might go to the top and take the Magic Mirror of the Babylonians and put it in the hands of the King."

"The King may be dead," Eean said, "or else he may be in such a state that he cannot see or hear any more."

We were then sitting under the greatest of the cedar trees, and he was eating pomegranates from my lap. I looked from out the shade of the cedar tree, and I saw the King of Babylon walking in his gardens.

The King was fearful; he looked to the right and to the left as he went on. When he saw a little deer that was standing still he was startled, and he turned back. As he came near the cedar tree he saw me standing there before him. I prostrated myself and I said, "O King, fear not for Babylon. The tower has not yet fallen, and the Magic Mirror will yet be placed in your hands." But the King only said, "Go to the tower and bring back to me the black cock that I tied to a board but did not sacrifice." Thereupon the King went within the palace.

I called upon Eean to come, and we went down the Way of the Lions, and through the Gate of Brass, and out into the city. It was the Hour of the Market, but there were no people in the market place. We went on, Eean and I, and we came before the tower. There we saw a throng such as would have filled many markets, and they were standing round and gazing at the tower.

I had never looked before on the Tower of Babylon. It was built tower upon tower to the height of four towers, and its color was red. Around the whole height of it went a stairway showing steps on this side and that as it went winding around. On the top of the topmost tower I saw a gleam, and I knew it was the Magic Mirror of the Babylonians.

That gleam dazzled me and put into my mind the thought of going to the top of the tower. I, out of all that throng, would go and bring down the Magic Mirror! I went among them, and they let me pass, for I had on me now the dress of one who belonged to the palace. I stood before the throng and I saw where a great space of rock was worn smooth—it was the rock against which Harut and Marut had lain.

I came to the first steps of the tower, and I climbed three of them. I heard the murmur of those who spoke of me, and I stood still. Then up the first round of the steps I went, keeping my mind from the thought of the great height that was above me. I came at last to where the second tower grew from the top of the first, and I stood and looked down, and I saw that the men below had already become little. It was then that I felt terror of the height that was above me.

I began to climb the steps of the second tower, fearful to look down and fearful to think of the number of steps that were before me. I went on and up, all in a terrible silence, and feeling that at the step above me something unbelievable would happen.

After a great length of time I came out on the space that was the top of the second tower. On that breadth I rested. As I waited there the coldness of death seemed to come over me.

But the coldness passed, and I felt the air again. I found the steps that went up and around the third of the towers. As I went on I felt that those steps leaned down on me and crushed me, and that with my feet alone I never could surmount them. Then I went down on my hands and knees and I climbed and climbed until my hands were bruised and the parts behind my knees ached. I thought that suddenly the steps would cease to be, and that I should find no place for my hands, and that thereupon I would fall down all the height I had climbed up. But step came after step, and at last I came out on the space that was the top of the third tower.

Above me was the fourth tower. I stood holding myself against it, and I looked down all the distance

I had climbed. I saw the great river shining whitely, and like pebbles in the bed of a river were the throngs below. But now my fear went from me. The silence was all around me, but I was exultant because of the silence through which I climbed. The height troubled me no more, rather it made me exultant, making me feel as the eagle feels. I came out on the top of the fourth tower, and there was nothing above me except the silent sky.

And there was the Magic Mirror of the Babylonians. It rested against the great spear that was Nimrod's, and it was turned toward the city and toward the King's palace.

I looked into the Magic Mirror. As I looked into it I saw a writing come upon it. I read the writing, and it said: *Bring the Magic Mirror of the Babylonians to the King of Babylon, but burden yourself not with the Spear of Nimrod.*

And that writing faded, and another writing appeared on the mirror. And the writing read: *Zabulun the Enchanter has been brought by Harut and Marut into the cave that is below the sea. For forty days they will watch over him, but then they will fall into a slumber. Zabulun will come forth from the cave that is beneath the sea, and in anger he will pursue him*

who revealed his plan for the taking of the Magic Mirror. Take one of the rings that are around the mirror. It will reveal when Zabulun comes from the cave, and it will show how near he comes in his pursuit of Eean, the boy who was apprenticed to him.

That writing faded, and I saw the rings that were around the mirror. I loosened one and I took it off the mirror and I put it around the wrist of my hand. The color of the ring changed to the green of the sea.

I took the Magic Mirror in my hands and I went down the stairway. Down I went, from the fourth to the third, and from the third to the second of the towers. As I went down the stairway around the first of the towers I heard the murmurs of the throng. High above my head I raised the Magic Mirror, and I went toward them holding it so.

And as I went among the throng I heard a voice cry out, "The tower trembles, the tower rocks." It was the voice of Eean. As the cry arose the throngs drew back from before the tower. They ran, and I ran carrying the mirror, and Eean ran beside me. And when we came to the market place we two were alone.

We stood in the empty market place and we looked toward the Tower of Babylon. In its great height it stood there, strong and wonderful. I heard the shouting of people around it. Then I saw the great tower swing like a child's swing. Dust rose up, cloud after cloud, and cloud over cloud. The cries of people came from out the clouds.

We stood there until we saw the sun shine through a cloud of dust. Then we knew that the Tower of Babylon was indeed fallen. Never again did we go near the place, but from travelers I have heard that where the tower stood there is emptiness, and that great blocks of stone are scattered far and wide.

HOW EEAN AND BIRD-OF-GOLD WENT FROM BABYLON

WE went into the King's gardens, carrying with us the Magic Mirror of the Babylonians. We saw the great cedar tree, and we went and sat under its branches and spoke of what we should do. The Magic Mirror would have to be given to the King, but for long Eean was fearful of going into the palace.

At last we went to the doors. They were unguarded, and we went within the palace. We came to the chamber where the King was accustomed to sit upon his throne, and we saw the King there. Around him there were bearded men with fierce eyes; by their fashion of carrying swords we knew them to be the leaders of the King's armies. These fierce-eyed men stood with their feet upon the steps of the throne, speaking in anger to the King. They did not see us as we came into the chamber. But in a while one caught sight of us, and he uttered a fierce word. I went to them, holding the Magic Mirror raised in my hands. The King raised his head, and he saw the mirror, and he cried out to us.

I went and left the Magic Mirror on the throne, beside the King. I lifted my voice and I told him how I had taken the mirror from the top of the tower, and that now the tower was overthrown, but the mirror was saved for the Babylonians. Then the King said to the fierce-eyed men, "This is the Magic Mirror of the Babylonians, and I say to you that Babylon is yet in safety." Again he said to them, "Speak now and say what is to be done about this girl who brought the mirror down from the tower."

One of the fierce-eyed men said, "Who is the boy with her?"

The King looked on Eean and knew who he was.

He said, "This is the boy who was with the Enchanter on whom be evil."

The man said, "Banish the girl and the boy also, but do no evil to them inasmuch as they have brought to us the Magic Mirror of the Babylonians."

The King said, "Take them from the city, but let some treasure be given to them because they have brought to me the Magic Mirror of the Babylonians."

One of the fierce-eyed men took us, and he brought us into a chamber in which there were many open jars. In some of the jars there were gold and in others there were silver coins. The fierce-eyed man who was with us spoke to me, and he said I might take from the jar with the gold coins. I took many of them, and I tied them in different parts of my dress. Then he bade us follow him, and he led us out of the palace and to a place where a chariot with two horses was standing.

He put Eean and me into the chariot, and he ordered the charioteer to drive with us out of the city. The charioteer, a silent man, stood up in his chariot and lashed the horses. We drove through one street, and then another and another street, and all the streets were empty. The charioteer called to the guards of a gateway, and the gate was opened, and we passed out of the city. We drove on until we came to where there was a great river. Then the charioteer halted, and he called across the river, and a man with a ferry came from the other side. He was a very ancient man, and he had a beard of great length. The charioteer said to him, "Old Man of the River, take these two across and away from us!"

We went into the ferry, and the ferryman took his pole and pushed across to the other side of the river. The man in the chariot turned his horses and drove back to Babylon.

When the ferryman had left us on the other side of the river, Eean said to me, "Where now shall we go?" I made answer and said, "We shall go to my country, and to the place where my father is. And it may be that Zabulun when he comes from the cave that is under the sea will not be able to find you there."

HOW EEAN AND BIRD-OF-GOLD WERE PURSUED BY ZABULUN THE ENCHANTER AND HOW THEY WENT TO THE CAVE OF CHIRON THE CENTAUR

O KING of the Western Island, our wanderings began on the day when the ferryman left us on the farther side of the river. We went to the country where my father dwelt. We found the old man still gathering brambles and thorns for his livelihood, and out of the treasure that had been given me I gave him riches, and he had not to go thorn-and-bramble gathering any more.

We had only been a little time in the hut that my father built when a new color came upon the ring I had taken off the Magic Mirror. Its color had been sea green, but now a red line came across it. By that we knew that Zabulun the Enchanter had left the cave that was under the sea. And the red line began to grow over the sea green of the ring, and we knew by this sign that he had begun to follow on our traces. Then said Eean to me, "I will go from this place and seek a hiding, and it may be that I shall baffle Zabulun who follows me." I said to Eean, "I shall go with you where you go." "Nay," said Eean, "it is not on your account that Zabulun pursues us. He has no rage or hatred against you, O Bird-of-Gold, and if I should go from this place by myself you would not be troubled by him."

Then I said to him, "O Eean, I had no playmate or companion until I met you in the King's gardens. Now I could not bear to see you go from me, and where you go I shall go too."

Afterward I asked him if there were in the world any Enchanters who were as powerful as Zabulun. He told me of Chiron the Centaur, and of Hermes Trismegistus, the wise Egyptian, and of Merlin whose home is on an island that is west of your Western Island. I thought that only from one of these Enchanters might we get aid against Zabulun.

The red grew over the sea green of the ring, and we knew that the further the red grew the nearer did Zabulun approach us. I wondered how we might get to one of the great Enchanters. Hermes Trismegistus, being in Egypt, was far, and Merlin, on the island beyond the Western Island, was farther still. I thought of Chiron the Centaur, and it seemed to me that him we might be able to find.

Now my father had lived a long time in the world, and he had heard many things, and he had thought over the things he had heard in the years when he had gathered brambles and thorns in the wilderness. I went to my father for word of Chiron the Centaur.

"Chiron the Centaur dwells all alone in a cave that is in the side of a mountain. The mountain is covered all over with a deep and an ancient forest," my father told me. And again he said, "Once I knew the direction in which that mountain is, and tomorrow I shall go into the wilderness, and as I walk about it may be that memory of it will come back to me."

He came back from the wilderness in the evening and he said, "Away toward where the morning star shines there is a great waste. If one skirts this waste one comes to a river the waters of which are as cold as snow. The river flows down from the mountain on the side of which is the cave of Chiron the Centaur. All this I heard in the days of my youth."

Over more and more of the sea green of the ring the red had grown. By this sign we knew that Zabulun was coming close to us. I spoke to Eean and I said that we both should make ready to go to the cave of Chiron the Centaur. Then when the morning star shone very brightly we took leave of my father and we went toward where it shone.

We came to the great waste, and we skirted it as we had been told. On we went, and we came to the rivers, the waters of which were cold as snow. We turned our faces toward the place from which the river flowed until we saw a mountain that was all covered with forest.

Deep and ancient and silent was that upward-growing forest. So frightened of its silence were we that we never let go of each other's hands. For days we went seeking the cave, and at last we heard cries— they might have been from birds, they might have been from the winds—that said, "Who comes to trouble the rest of Chiron the ancient Centaur?"

We went toward where the cries came from and we saw the mouth of the cave. We followed the track that led to it, and in fear we went within.

And there was Chiron the ancient Centaur. His head and his breast, his shoulders and his arms were a man's, and his body and his feet and his tail were a horse's. His great beard was white, and his horse's body was shrunken, but his eyes were like pools in which there are living fires. The power of all the kings in the world was in his eyes.

Chiron lay beside a fire in which fragrant woods burned. He turned his eyes upon it, and we heard cries as if the winds in the cave made them, "Who

comes to trouble the rest of Chiron the ancient Centaur?"

I went down on my knees and I beseeched him, "O Chiron, wisest of all who deal in enchantments," I said, "there is one named Zabulun, an evil Enchanter, who pursues us. We have come to beg you to tell us how we may escape him."

"Not to me should you have come," the voice of Chiron boomed out. "What have I to do with men who are as far from wisdom as Zabulun? Only one who is like him may strive with him. Go to another, go to another."

"To whom shall we go, O Centaur?" I asked.

"Hermes Trismegistus in Egypt is nearer to Zabulun than I am. Go to him, and he may tell you how to baffle Zabulun. Tell him that you have seen the Phoenix in the cave of Chiron the Centaur."

As he said this there flew into the cave the great bird that is called the Phoenix. I may not describe her to you, O King. She flew to the fire of fragrant-smelling woods and she held herself above it. She fanned the flame with her wings, and the fire rose up and caught her breast. Then the bird sank down on the fire, and we saw her burn under the eyes of Chiron the Centaur. The flame died out, and what we saw of the bird that burned, and the wood that made the fire, was a heap of ashes.

Then out of that heap of ashes came a bird. It was smaller than the bird that burned, but more radiant. As the bird stayed with the ashes beneath her feet she grew by some great thing that was within her, and then she rose over the ashes and fanned them with her wings. Again I looked upon the Phoenix.

"Go to Hermes Trismegistus in Egypt, and tell him that you saw the long-lived Phoenix burn herself in the cave of Chiron the Centaur and come again out of the burning. And when you tell this to Hermes in Egypt he will tell you what you may do to make yourself free of Zabulun."

The Phoenix flew from the cave. Then Chiron turned his eyes upon us and he spoke to us of the way we should go to find Hermes Trismegistus in Egypt. When he had told us all we went backward out of his cave, and then turned and went through the depths of the silent forest, taking the way the Centaur bade us take.

HOW EEAN AND BIRD-OF-GOLD CAME TO HERMES TRISMEGISTUS IN EGYPT

WE found a ship, and I paid for the voyage out of the riches I had, and we came to Egypt. The ring upon my hand showed that we were now far away from the one who pursued us, from Zabulun the Enchanter.

But we two lost our way in Egypt, and we wandered about, reaching nowhere. Then Zabulun gained upon us again, as the ring showed. We hid in a village by the river, and we stayed there until the season when the cranes fly overhead on their way to Ethiopia.

Then we went from that village, and we came again upon the way that had been lost. We followed that way and we came to the great pyramid in which Hermes Trismegistus had his cell. Down into the deepest chamber we went, and we came before Hermes the Egyptian.

He sat before a table that was of diamond and that had wonderful figures upon it. He was youthful, and light seemed to come from his forehead. As wonderful

as the eyes of Chiron was the brow of Hermes Trismegistus.

We knelt at the threshold of his cell, and I said, "O
thrice-great Hermes! We have been in the cave of
Chiron the Centaur, and we have seen the long-lived
Phoenix burn herself to ashes, and come out of the
ashes more radiant than before. Chiron was kind to
us, and he sent us to you, O thrice-great Hermes. We
are pursued by an Enchanter whose name is Zabulun,
and we have come to beseech you to tell us how we
may make ourselves free from him."

Hermes Trismegistus said, "I know of Zabulun, the
wrong-doing Enchanter. But what have I to do with
one who is so removed from wisdom?"

I beseeched him again, saying, "Save us from this
wrong-doing Enchanter who would destroy us. He
has come near us often, and he will assuredly overtake us if you do not give us help, O thrice-great
Hermes."

Then Hermes said, "Near the Western Island there
dwells an Enchanter whose name is Merlin. Not one
of the great Enchanters is he, nor like to Chiron or
myself, for he chooses to love rather than to be wise.
He is nearer to Zabulun than we are, but yet he is not
a wrong-doing Enchanter. Go to Merlin and say to

him that you have been within the cell of Hermes Trismegistus, and that you have learned from him the answer to the riddle that the Sphinx asks, and Merlin will show you how you both may be saved from Zabulun, the wrong-doing Enchanter.

"But to come to Merlin's island, which is west of the Western Island, you will have first to go among the Atlantes, who live by the Western Ocean. They eat no living thing and they never have dreams. When you come to them, seek out the wisest among them, and ask him to tell you of Merlin, and of how you may come to him.

"To come to the Atlantes you will have to pass by the Sphinx in the desert. Few ever pass her, for she has a riddle that she asks of every one. And the one who cannot answer her riddle is torn to pieces by the Sphinx. But I shall tell you the answer to give to the riddle that the Sphinx asks."

Then Hermes, thrice-great Hermes, told us the Sphinx's riddle and the answer that we should make to it. He told us the way we should go to pass by the Sphinx and come to the people that are called the Atlantes. We left the cell of Hermes, and passed out of the pyramid, and went on our way.

We came to where the great Sphinx stretches herself out in the sand, and by the light of a great moon we saw her lion's paws and her woman's face. We heard the purring sound that comes through the lips of the Sphinx, and we halted between her paws.

"What is Man?" said the Sphinx, asking her riddle.

The paws that stretched alongside of us were quiet, and the voice of the Sphinx was very quiet. We saw her face far above us, and it was calm, though there was much scorn and fierceness in it.

"What is Man?" said the Sphinx.

Then I replied as Hermes Trismegistus had taught me to reply, "Man is he whose Mother is the Earth and whose Father is the Stars."

"Go," said the Sphinx.

Then we clambered across the great paws of the Sphinx, and we went on our way. Along the border of the desert we went, and when the great moon had changed herself to a little moon that was hardly to be seen in the sky we came among the Atlantes, the people who eat no living thing and who never have dreams.

The ring showed us that Zabulun, the wrong-doing Enchanter, had not drawn near us for many days. We were far away from him when we came among the Atlantes. But soon he came near us again. By that time I had found him who was wisest among this people, and I asked him to tell me of Merlin, and of how I might come to him.

"Not often does the island on which Merlin dwells show itself," said he who was wisest among the Atlantes. "On the mid day of summer it is to be seen. Then it draws near to the Western Island, and if you will cast upon the water nine cocks' combs and four peacocks' feathers, Merlin will let you come upon his island."

Thereupon he who was wisest among them gave us the nine cocks' combs and four peacocks' feathers. They reverenced Hermes of Egypt, the people that are called the Atlantes, and because we had spoken with Hermes and had been in his cell, they brought us on board a ship that had great leathern sails, and in that ship they carried us to your island, O King.

HOW EEAN AND BIRD-OF-GOLD CAME TO KING MANUS'S STABLES

WE came to your island, O King (said Bird-of-Gold, continuing her story), but no sooner did we step from the ship to the landing stones than we suffered a loss. The ring that was around my wrist broke and fell into the sea, and thereafter we had no sign that would show how close the evil Zabulun was in pursuit of us.

We set off for that part of the land that Merlin's island comes near to. One day our way was through a dark valley, and we lay down there to sleep. I awakened after some hours of slumber, and I looked toward Eean, and I saw that he was still sleeping. I left him to his sleep, but when hours passed I went over to awaken him. But I could not awaken him from that slumber, do what I would. For three days and three nights he slept in that valley while I watched beside him.

At last he awoke saying, "What day is this, and how near is Zabulun to us?" I told him that we were two days from the mid day of summer, and that we had no sign now to show us how close the Enchanter might be. We were greatly troubled, O King, for we knew not how we might come to Merlin's island by the mid day of summer.

It was then that we heard of your horses, King Manus. We were told of their swiftness, and we said to each other, "Only by the speed of these horses can we reach the place that Merlin's island comes near, and by Merlin's aid save ourselves from the power of Zabulun, the wrong-doing Enchanter."

At nightfall we came before your palace and your stable. Now it was not hard for us to open the doors of your stable. Your watchers drank of a drug that I made, O King. Eean brought a cup to them, and they, thinking the drink had been sent to them from your supper table, drank it. At once they fell into a slumber. Then we opened the four locks of the iron door with the keys that were in their belts. Eean went within the stable while I kept watch at the gate of the orchard.

Alas, Eean was taken before he could mount the white horse, and before I went to take the bridle of the red one. I saw him being brought within the palace, and I saw two new watchers take their places beside the door.

For a long time I stood in the shadow of the orchard gate not knowing what to do. Then I thought that I should still take one of the horses and go to the place where Merlin might be spoken to, and so win aid for Eean, my beloved companion. I made another drug, and I put it into a drink, and I brought the cup to those who were at the stable door. These, too, were unsuspecting; they thought I had brought it from the supper table, and they drank, and they, too, lost their senses.

Then I opened the iron door of the stable the way we had opened it before and I went within. I saw the red horse in his stall and I put my hand upon his neck. As I did this the black horse broke loose, and he plunged at me, and he caught me by the flesh of the shoulders and he flung me down. He reared above me, and was about to bring his hoofs crashing down upon me. Then indeed I should have been trampled to death but that you and your men came in, O King.

You came with torches and you drove that fierce black horse away from my body. Never was I in such danger of death as I was in then. I do not think I am now in such danger as when I lay under the feet of that fierce black horse. But it is for you to judge, O King.

Bird-of-Gold finished her story, and, closing her eyes, she laid her head upon her hands. All at that supper table looked toward King Manus. Eean seemed to hear nothing of her story, for all the time his eyes were upon the King's face.

Said King Manus, "She has been in danger as great as the danger she is in now, for verily, that black horse of mine is a manslayer. The girl, too, shall go free."

Then the King drank another cup of wine and was silent for a while. Then he spoke again, saying: "They have fled a great way, these two. I should not be glad if they lost the match with this Zabulun. By the open hand of my father, they may take my two horses, the white one and the red one, and ride to that part of the Western Island that Merlin's island comes near. For payment to me, let them ask Merlin the Enchanter what moves I should make in that game of chess that, for half my lifetime, I have been playing with King Connal."

When King Manus said this the last binding was taken off Eean and off Bird-of-Gold, and they went to him and they kissed his hands. Eean promised that they would bring the horses back to the stable, and he promised, too, that he would ask Merlin about the moves in the game of chess, and would bring back the answer to the King.

In the middle of it all, one of the stewards came to the King, and said there was one in the palace who knew the youth Eean and who could not be withheld from coming to him. As they were speaking about him, he came into the supper room, an old man, whom they all recognized as the one who watched before the door of the King's chamber, to prevent those who came with requests that might not be granted being brought before the King.

He went straight to where Eean stood, and holding up a torch he looked upon him. He no sooner looked than he cried out, "It is he—indeed, indeed it is he!" And Eean, his hands grasping the old man, said, "It is Anluan! It is my father!"

Then it was told to Eean how Anluan had left the nets of a fisherman after his son had gone with Zabulun as his apprentice; and it was told, too, how he had come to the palace, and how he had been made the officer at the King's doorway on account of his extraordinary patience, a patience that he had learned when he handled the net, and that wore out the most insistent of those who came with requests to the King.

There was much rejoicing over the meeting between Eean and his father Anluan. Then Anluan turned to her whose hand Eean held, to Bird-of-Gold, and having wept over her he began to question her about her accomplishments. It was at this point that the stewards took Anluan away, for the pair had now to make ready for their ride to that part of the Western Island that Merlin's island came near to on the mid day of summer which would be the morrow of that very night. Refreshments were given them at the King's table, the newest of meats and the oldest of wines. Then they went out of the hall, and they mounted the horses that the grooms of King Manus now brought out for them, Eean taking the white horse, and Bird-of-Gold the red horse. A bound and a bound, and the white and the red started off, spurning the cobblestones of the courtyard, riding toward their meeting with that Enchanter who would give them freedom from Zabulun, Merlin, the Enchanter of the Isle of Britain.

PART THREE

The Two Enchanters

The Two Enchanters

MERLIN AND VIVIEN

A GREAT Enchanter indeed was Merlin. He served with his enchantments the King of the Isle of Britain from the time he was a stripling to the time when he was two score years of age. Then, when he might have passed from being a lesser to being a great Enchanter, Merlin vanished altogether and was seen no more at the court of the King of the Isle of Britain. All the great works he had planned were left undone, all the instruments he had gathered were left unused, all the books he had brought together were left unopened, and the King whom he had served so long was left without an Enchanter.

If there were one to blame for that it was the daughter of King Dionas. She was young, but she was ungentle. What she saw, that she would have.

One day a stranger was passing with her father, and when he looked on her he said, "A young hawk she is, a young hawk that has not yet flown at any prey." That very day the daughter of King Dionas walked on the plain that was at a distance from her father's castle. The stranger who had spoken of her to her father was there also, and he looked long upon her.

"Who art thou who lookest on me so?" said the child.

"Thou art Nimiane, who art also called Vivien," said the stranger.

"Yea," said she, "but who art thou, man?"

"I am called Merlin," he said, "and I am the Enchanter to the King of the Isle of Britain."

"Show me thine enchantments," said Vivien, who feared not to speak to any man.

Now Merlin had looked on all the ladies who were at the court of the King of the Isle of Britain, and on the maidens who were in far countries and distant castles, and besides, the ladies of the times of old had been shown him in his Magic Glass, but never before had he seen any one who seemed so lovely to him as this child. She was bright-eyed as a bird. She had a slim body, and pale cheeks, and quick, quick hands.

Her hair was red and in thick tangles. "Show me thine enchantments," she cried to him again.

Merlin bade her come with him and she came. He brought her to a high place, a place that was of rock with rocks piled all about it. On the ground he made magical figures. Then he said magical words. And all the time Vivien, slim Vivien with her tangle of red hair, stood upon the rocks with her eyes upon him.

Upon the ground that was all rock Merlin made a garden with roses blowing and clear waters flowing, with birds singing among the leaves and fishes swimming in the streams. He made trees grow, too, with honey-tasting fruits upon them.

Vivien went through the garden, plucking the flowers and tasting the fruits that grew there. She turned to Merlin and looked at him again with her bright eyes. "Canst thou make a castle for me?" said she.

Then Merlin made his magical figures and said his magical words over again. The stones that were strewn about everywhere came together and built themselves up into a castle. When the castle rose before them Vivien took Merlin by the hand, and they went through its doorway and up the stairway and into the castle turret. And when they looked from the turret Vivien said, "Would that no one should know of this garden and this castle but thou and I!"

He told her that the castle and the garden would be hidden. Then when they were leaving the garden he put a mist all around, a mist that those who came that way could not see through and were made fearful of venturing into.

And so the castle and the garden were all unknown to men. But Vivien would come, passing through the mist, and going into the garden and up into the turret. At first she would not have Merlin near her. Afterward it came to pass that she would summon him. A bugle hung in the turret of the castle, and she would blow upon it, and he would come and stay by her.

He was two score years of age, and she was five years less than a score. Nevertheless he thought it better to watch her dancing with bright green leaves in her red hair than to know all that would bring him from being a lesser to being a great Enchanter. Of the maidens and great ladies he had seen, some, he told her, were like light, and some were like flowers, and some were like a flame of fire. But she, he said, was like the wind. And he thought no more upon the King of the Isle of Britain, nor on the great work he was to do for him, and he spent his days in watching

Vivien, and in listening to Vivien, and in making magic things for Vivien's delight.

Her father once took her away from the place near where the hidden garden and the hidden castle stood. Vivien was in another country now. And when she went among those who were strangers to her she found out that nothing mattered to her except the looks and the words of Merlin. The castle and the garden—she did not think of them, nor of the magic things he had made for her. Her thoughts were only on Merlin, who was so wise and who could do such wonders.

When she came back, and when she met him in the hidden garden, she caught hold of his hands, and she would not let go of them. Nor would she tell Merlin why this change had come over her, and why she would keep close to him now and not apart. At last she said to him, "What ladies and what maidens have you known, O my master Merlin?"

Then Merlin took his Magic Glass into his hands, and in it he showed her all the ladies who were at the court of the King of the Isle of Britain, and he showed her all the lovely maidens who lived in far countries and in distant castles whom he knew. Vivien threw herself on the ground with her face to the rock after she had looked into the Magic Glass.

Then afterward she watched him in a way different from the way she had watched him before. What he said and what he did she remembered well. Soon she understood his magic figures and could make them. She came to understand his magic words and to be able to repeat them. And Merlin would say to her, "O my little hawk, fly at this—and this—and this."

One day as they wandered through a forest Vivien asked him to tell her the mightiest spell that he knew. The Enchanter told it to her. She stood still, with all her quick mind in her face, while he put aside the tangles of her red hair and spoke into her ear.

It was a spell that would hold in a place the one whom it was spoken over. When he had told her he went at her bidding and seated himself under a forest tree. Vivien, laughing, made a magic circle around him and repeated the spell that he had given her. When she did this the Enchanter was enchanted. Merlin stayed under the forest tree, and there he would stay, for he could not move until the spell that was said over him was unsaid by Vivien.

And Vivien danced around him, her red hair shaking, her bright eyes gleaming, her quick hands waving. She called to him, "Merlin, Merlin Enchanter, come to me." But Merlin, under the forest tree, could not move. She ran through the woods and he could not follow after her. In a while she came back and stood beside him.

Said Merlin to her, "Why have you worked this spell upon me, and why have you left me here so that I cannot move?" She knelt down on the ground beside where he sat.

"O Merlin," said she, "I would leave you here enchanted, for fear you should leave me and go among the maidens and the ladies who are so lovely." And when she said that her face was so hard that he knew she would hold him there.

But Merlin smiled, and he said to her, "I would stay always where you are, Vivien, blossom of the furze."

"Nay," said she, "you would go from me. Why should you not? You have great works to do for the King of the land. And when you see again the ladies and the maidens who are the loveliest in the world you will not come back again to Vivien. I shall hate the castle and the garden that you made for me, and I shall hate every one who will come near me. I shall hold you, Merlin, here, even until the wolves come out at night and devour you and me."

"I will build a castle for you in an empty country,

and no one shall ever be there but you and me," said Merlin.

"Nay," said Vivien, "they will search the world for you, Merlin, and when they find you, you will have to go with them."

Then Merlin, as if it were a magic thing that would please her, brought out his thought about the Island of the White Tower. Away beyond the Western Island, in a sea that is never sailed on, that island lies. Only on Midsummer Day does it come near to the Western Island so that men may see it. There, said Merlin, they might go. Those who would search for him could never come to him there. He told her more and more about the Island of the White Tower, and Vivien listened in delight to all he told her. And when he had sworn he would take her to it she unsaid the spell with which she had bespelled him, and he rose up from where he had been held, and he sprang across the magic circle that was drawn upon the ground. And with Vivien Merlin went through the forest.

The fishermen who cast their nets by the shores of the Western Ocean have this story of Merlin and Vivien. They tell how in a boat of crystal twelve creatures sailed to the Island of the White Tower. Two were Merlin and Vivien, and nine were the nine prime bards of the Isle of Britain who went with Merlin, and one was the tame wolf that was Merlin's servant. They sailed out upon a Midsummer's Day, and from that good day to this no hint or hair of the Enchanter has been seen by king nor clown in all the Isle of Britain.

ZABULUN THE ENCHANTER

IT was Anluan, the father of Eean, Anluan who had once been a fisherman by the shores of the Western Ocean, who told this story of the Enchanter of the Isle of Britain. The fishermen know the story, and they, more often than any others, have seen the Island of the White Tower as it shows itself on the rim of the Western Ocean.

The story was told after the white horse and the red horse had clattered across the stones of the courtyard, bringing Eean and Bird-of-Gold toward their meeting with Merlin. Candles thicker than a man's wrist had been put upon the supper table, fresh torches had been set in the sconces along the walls, and logs of resinous wood had been piled upon the hearth. All this was done so that the King and his lords might drink their last cups of wine before they went into the sleeping chambers.

And now, in the light of shining candles and blazing torches and mounting hearth fires, the squires and the servers went among the company, filling the wine cups up. Some already had the wine in their cups and were waiting for King Manus to raise his in a toast. Then the strangest of strange things happened. No wind came into the hall, but suddenly the candles upon the table and the torches along the walls went out. The servers went to relight the torches at the hearth, but the hearth blaze had died down, and all the logs were black.

And blackness was in the chamber where, a minute before, candles and torches and hearth fires were blazing. The King and his lords stood around the table, while the servers and squires ran through every chamber of the castle to find a spark of light.

But not even a spark could they find; not the light of a rush candle even was to be found in any hall or chamber in the castle. And on every stairway the same story was told, how suddenly light and fire had gone black out.

But now the grooms came in with flints and steel and hemp. Every one tried to strike a spark, but no spark came for all their striking. And now, all over the castle, there were outbursts of woe: the cooks were lamenting that they would have no fires, and the women were weeping because lights could not be brought them. It was then that King Manus bade his lords stand around laying their hands upon the table.

The next thing was that a figure appeared at the doorway. All saw it, for there was a line of faint light around it. It was the figure of a tall man. "Speak," said King Manus with his hand stretched to the figure.

"If you will have me speak," said the man.

"The lights and the fires have been quenched in the castle. How has this come to be?"

"It is in the power of an Enchanter of the second degree to quench light and fire," said the man in the darkness. "Further, King Manus, the fire and light that are extinguished cannot be brought back until the Enchanter lifts his ban."

"Have you come to tell me this?" asked the King.

"I have come to make a request of you, King Manus," said the man in the darkness.

Then Anluan, the father of Eean, he whose duty it was to let none that might have a request come face

to face with the King, groped around the room that he might place himself before his master. But before he came to where King Manus stood the man with the line of light around had come so close that he and the King looked into each other's eyes.

"O King," said the stranger, "I have answered what you asked of me. Now I make my request. It is that the black horse that is in your stable be given to me."

There was a stir in the darkened hall, and then there was an outcry. It was from Anluan, the father of Eean. "O, King Manus, beware of the man who knows of the powers of Enchanters. He may be the one who would ride in chase of Eean, my son!"

"He has made a request of me," said King Manus. "By the open hand of my father, it will have to be granted him."

"It is for the one horse that can follow the others," Anluan cried.

"I have never refused a request! Alas, alas, in one night the three horses that were my pride are taken from me!"

"Strike now, and light candle and torch and hearth fire," said the one who had come among them.

Flint was struck upon steel; sparks came and made the hemp blaze; candle and torch and hearth fire were lighted again. Then all looked at the one who had come among them.

Tall he was, with a dark and bony face and eyes that were like a hawk's eyes. His dress was a plain cloak that had a hood that went over his head. And yet, although he had not the staff nor the robe of an Enchanter, it did not need Anluan's cry to tell the company that here was the one to whom his son had been apprenticed—Zabulun the Enchanter!

"Why do you go in chase of my son?" Anluan cried.

"Harut and Marut laid hands upon me. Am I to have no more mastery because of that?" said Zabulun. "For forty days I was laid in the cave that is under the sea, and do men think that all power is gone from me because of that? I thought all that time that what I worked for would come to pass, and that the Magic Mirror of Babylon would be lost in the ruin of the Tower of Babylon and that destruction would come upon the Babylonians. This would have been if the boy who was my apprentice had been faithful to me. But he spoke the words that restored the mirror to the Kings of Babylon. And I, whose name, as I thought, would stand forever as one who had worked a great destruction, am as naught—my name is a name to laugh at. And shall he pass from my mastership, the boy who let this befall me? Not so; he has still to be my aid. I have paid you, his father, gold for his seven years' service, and his service still belongs to me."

Then, turning to King Manus, Zabulun said, "You have granted my request. Command now that your grooms go to the stable and bring out the black horse that I am to ride."

King Manus gave the commands. Then out of the door of the castle they all went, and into the courtyard. The still light of the dawn, the dawn of Midsummer's Day, was coming over the world. The grooms went to the stable and, in full sight of all, unlocked the great stable door and brought out the black horse whose swiftness was such that he could overtake the wind of March that was before him, while the wind of March that was behind could not overtake him. They brought forth the black horse and they held him while the dark-faced man put himself astride. Then the hoofs of the last of the King's horses struck fire out of the stones of the courtyard, while a cry went up from Anluan.

And away went Zabulun the Enchanter—away, away in pursuit of Eean and Bird-of-Gold, and the light of the Midsummer Day came into the world.

THE LAST FLIGHT OF EEAN
AND BIRD-OF-GOLD

As the first light of the Midsummer Day came over the world the two who were fleeing before him were speaking of Zabulun the Enchanter. "That we may baffle him," one said.

"And what if we cannot baffle him this time?" said the other.

"Then he will take me and make me do terrible services for him"—it was Eean who said this—"and, worse than all the services he will make me do, he will separate us."

"No, no," said Bird-of-Gold. "If he takes us this time, I shall do everything to make myself useful to the Enchanter. I have thought out ways in which I can serve him. He will not separate us, and we will be together still."

"O Bird-of-Gold," said Eean, "I am fearful lest he should slay you for taking the Magic Mirror off the Tower of Babylon. But I have a sword, and he shall not harm you."

"I shall escape him," Bird-of-Gold said, "and as he

followed you and me across the world, so I shall follow him and you, and we shall never be apart."

They had learned in their wanderings all ways of guiding themselves, and as they galloped on they were heading for the Western Ocean. Darkness was around them at first. But the sky was wide and clear, and Bird-of-Gold, when she raised her head, could see and name the bright planets. There was Mars with his red pulse. Bird-of-Gold likened this planet to the steed that she rode, and as she rode on she sang to herself the song that the shepherd boys in her own country used to sing about another star:

> That star, I know, is Betelgeuse;
> Yet, as I walk the hills by day,
> I hardly know his splendid name—
> That star is far away.
>
> But when at night I travel on,
> Or watch across an empty land,
> Than Betelgeuse, my star of stars,
> No thing is nearer hand.
>
> Then send a ray that I may own
> The fortune that is mine:
> O Betelgeuse, my star of stars,
> My forehead's for your sign!

And after all the countries he had wandered through, Eean was now back on the ground of his own country. He heard the cry of the curlews overhead. He saw the lakes that looked as if even the birds had forgotten them, so lonely they were—lonely, but with deep memories. He saw the cairns of stones above the long-dead heroes. Once he saw a fox upon a cairn, and it seemed to him that this was the very fox he had chased away from his mother's coop the day before the Enchanter had taken him away from the Western Island.

With strong hearts King Manus's horses galloped on. But the heart of Eean was strained with the thought of the distance that was still before them. First, a great mountain had to be crossed, then a wide plain, then that other mountain from the top of which one could see the Western Ocean in the daylight. And Zabulun the Enchanter might come upon them in the hills or on the plain and say a word that might stop their horses' gallop.

But they came to the last mountain top, and they saw the waters of the Western Ocean with gleams of gold coming upon them. Down the heather-covered hillside their horses hurried. And as the broad sun rose over the broad ocean the hurrying feet of the white and the red horse were scattering the foam along the shore.

And as they watched they saw Merlin's island grow out of the dimness of the sea. Then the sun became fuller and it lighted up the White Tower, and Eean and Bird-of-Gold knew they had come to their journey's end indeed. They sprang off their horses, and they dipped their hands in the sea, and they kissed each other.

"Now we must cast over on the island the tokens that the Atlantes gave us," Eean said, "the cocks' combs and the peacocks' feathers. If they come to Merlin, he will let us cross to his island, and we can swim our horses over. But how shall we know if the tokens come to him?"

He raised the bag in which were the nine cocks' combs and the four peacocks' feathers. He cast the bag toward the island. Through the air it went like a flying bird.

They mounted their horses again, ready to swim them across when they got some signal from the island. And the signal came. It was the howl of the wolf that was Merlin's servant.

Now they were to swim their horses across. As they went into the water, Bird-of-Gold looked back. Down through the heather of the hillside a rider was coming. He was on a black horse. They knew him for Zabulun, the Enchanter from whom they were fleeing.

HOW EEAN WON HIS RELEASE FROM ZABULUN THE ENCHANTER

MERLIN, with the tame wolf that was his servant beside him, was standing by the White Tower on the morning of that Midsummer Day. And Vivien was upon the tower, singing to her colored birds and looking out over the sea.

Vivien, who played with her colored birds, had still the look of a child in her face. Her hair was no longer in tangles; it was softer than it was once, and it fell softly over her shoulders. Her eyes, for all the child's look that was in her face, were as if they had seen many things come and change and pass.

Like a King, or like one who had been always near a King, was Merlin the Enchanter. He smiled, and his smile was calm and royal. But one might have said that his eyes were strangely close to each other and that his lips were strangely red.

His beard was long and gray. He wore a white robe with a belt of green leaves around it, and a chaplet of oak leaves was on his head. Vivien was dressed in green, with a golden belt clasped around her, and with green leaves in her soft hair.

So they were standing by and on the tower, Merlin, Vivien, and Merlin's tame wolf, when the tokens that were from the Atlantes came. Merlin laid his hand upon the wolf, and the wolf gave the howl that was the signal for Eean and Bird-of-Gold to come on the Island of the White Tower. The Enchanter saw them ride their horses into the water. And then another token came to him—the token that one magician sends to another, a Bird of Foam it was, and Zabulun sent it.

Deep were the waters, but great-hearted were the horses of King Manus, the white horse and the red horse, and with Eean and Bird-of-Gold astride them they swam to the Island of the White Tower. They came to the sloping shore, and the riders helped the horses up to the hard ground. The white and the red horse stood shivering from their plunge into the ocean. Afterward they threw themselves on the grass and lay as still as if they were dead.

Not to the horses, but out to the sea did Eean and Bird-of-Gold look. The black horse with Zabulun astride him was swimming now. Swiftly to the White

Tower where they saw Merlin stand they went.

"O Merlin," Eean cried, "to you we have come to save us from the Enchanter who has pursued us from one end of the world to the other."

"From whom have you come, you who have sent such tokens?" said Merlin.

"From Hermes Trismegistus in his secret cell. And Hermes told us to say to you that we have heard from him the answer to the riddle that the Sphinx asks, and that we crossed the desert to come to you, answering the Sphinx."

"Who is the Magician who pursues you?"

"Zabulun, once a Prince in Babylon, O Merlin."

"Is it he who pursues you?—Zabulun! I shall have a welcome for Zabulun."

"Save us, O Merlin, from Zabulun," Bird-of-Gold cried.

Vivien came down from the tower. "It is Zabulun who comes to our island in chase of these two, my Vivien," Merlin said. "Now you shall see me match my power with Zabulun's."

"A match between magicians, how entertaining it will be!" cried Vivien, clapping her hands.

"O lady, if Zabulun is not baffled it will be death or separation for us," said Bird-of-Gold to her.

"Merlin will baffle him—you will find that Merlin

will baffle him," said Vivien. "You see, he has done nothing to impress me for an age."

Now Merlin had sent the tame wolf that was his servant upon an errand, and the wolf at this moment returned leading nine men who wore white robes and who had chaplets of oak leaves upon their brows. These were the nine prime bards of the Isle of Britain who had come to the Island of the White Tower with Merlin, their chief.

They stood as he told them, four on one side and five on the other, with the Enchanter of the Isle of Britain between them. Merlin told Eean to stand with the four bards. He touched them with his staff, and the row of bards and Eean with them became all as alike as ten peas in a pea pod. And Merlin went to Bird-of-Gold and touched her also, and she became like the lady Vivien exactly.

Now the black horse that bore Zabulun came to the sloping bank of the Island of the White Tower, and Zabulun sprang off his back and drew the black horse up on the bank. The horse breathed mightily, and then like the others lay down on the grass.

With great and sure strides Zabulun came to the White Tower where Merlin stood. "Hail, Merlin," he cried in a loud voice.

"Hail, Zabulun."

"You know of an apprentice of mine who has come to your island."

"Find him, O mighty magician."

Zabulun looked and saw the ten men who looked exactly alike, and the two women whom one could not tell one from the other. He turned to Merlin then and he said, "What a simple trick you would play upon me! Nine bards you have, and there are ten before us. One of them is Eean, the boy apprenticed to me."

"Then you will take him, Zabulun."

It is certain that Merlin did not think that Zabulun would do what he did now. He changed himself into a hound. Running among the ten that were there he sniffed at them. By the smell of the horse he had ridden he would find Eean.

But as he ran among them Merlin touched each of the nine bards and Eean with them with his staff. They all became pigeons and flew up into the air. One had a feather awry. This was Eean on whom Zabulun had laid a paw just as he was being transformed.

Instantly Zabulun changed himself into a hawk and strove to rise above the flock of pigeons. As he did he saw the one that had a feather awry. Over him he came.

Then Eean, seeing the hawk above him, dropped instantly to the earth. The others flew down with him, crowding around to hide the ruffled feather. They came before the door of Merlin's house. They flew in and lighted down on the floor while the hawk came sweeping up to the doorway.

Merlin touched the pigeons with his staff and again transformed them. They became ten rings of gold that lay upon the floor. As the hawk flew in and perched on a chair to fix his eyes upon them, the rings of gold rolled into the fire.

Then Zabulun transformed himself into a tongs and went hunting through the fire for the rings. He picked up one ring and flung it out on the floor, he picked up another ring and flung it out on the floor, and so on, until the ten rings were out of the fire. Merlin touched the rings with his staff, and they were transformed into ten grains of corn. Upon these ten grains Vivien and Bird-of-Gold threw handful after handful of grains of corn.

But now Zabulun changed himself into a cock with strong legs and wide claws and a hungry beak. With his claws he scratched through the heap of grain. With his beak he picked the grains up. Vivien and Bird-of-Gold kept throwing on the floor handful after handful of corn to cover the ten grains that were Eean and the nine bards.

But the beak of the cock went so fiercely and so hungrily among them that only a few grains more than the ten were left upon the floor when Vivien and Bird-of-Gold found out they had no more handfuls to fling. Then it seemed as if the cock with his sharp eye would soon pick out the grain that was Eean.

Then with his staff Merlin touched nine of the grains, leaving one untouched. The one he left untouched was Eean. The nine were changed into weasels, and they faced the cock fiercely. Then was Zabulun startled. Instead of picking at the grain that was Eean he fluttered up from the ground and went out of the door of the house.

Merlin touched the grain that was left and Eean stood up. Bird-of-Gold clapped her hands for joy on seeing him again. But Eean ran out of the door of the house after the cock that was Zabulun the Enchanter. He snatched up a strong staff as he ran.

Zabulun had changed back into his own form. But now Eean had no fear of him. He ran toward him. And Zabulun took up a staff that was lying there and made to defend himself.

Then began the battle between Eean and Zabulun.

Eean struck at Zabulun, and Zabulun struck at Eean, and each defended himself with the staff that he had. They fought their way across the island, from one side to the other. They fought until their staves were broken and until they were covered with bruises. Then they threw away their staves and gripped one another. All around the island they wrestled. Strong were the hands of Zabulun. Eean felt his own hands were strong upon Zabulun, and yet he could not throw him. Soon Eean lost sense of everything except two gripping and rocking figures.

They wrestled their way across the island, down to the shore where they had landed and where the three horses of King Manus were lying. They wrestled until the sea water came over their feet. Again things became clear to Eean. He knew that if he could overthrow the Enchanter he would win his freedom.

He fastened upon Zabulun a grip that seemed to be stronger than his own life. He heaved with a power that seemed to bring up his last breath. He bent Zabulun over. He brought him down, his head in the water. He flung himself upon the prone Enchanter.

"What would you have of me?" Zabulun said at last.

"Release. Say you have no more mastership of me."

"I say it. I have no more mastership of you. You have release from me."

"I let you rise."

Then Eean took his grip off Zabulun. The Enchanter rose up and took himself out of the water.

So Zabulun was defeated, and so release was given to Eean, the Boy Apprenticed to the Enchanter. Zabulun mounted the black horse that was, King Manus's and had him swim the water. He rode across the plain and over one mountain and another mountain until he came to the castle of King Manus. There he left the horse to neigh for his grooms.

What became of Zabulun afterward is not written in the book that is the History of the Enchanters. Some say that from that Midsummer's Day he ceased to be named with the great Enchanters. The powers he had gained, they say, shrank from him. Afterward a famous juggler appeared in the world. He used to go into the halls of Kings on festival nights and do marvelous feats with balls and rings and knives, and play music on all manner of instruments, going from King's castle to King's castle. That juggler, they say— but they may be mistaken—was Zabulun, once Prince of Babylon, and once master of the Inaccessible Island.

Eean and Bird-of-Gold went within the White Tower and conversed from noon to dusk with Merlin and the lady Vivien. Before that Midsummer's Day had passed into darkness, they mounted the white steed and the red steed and had them swim across the waters. When they came to the farther shore they let the horses stand for a while. Then mounting them again they rode over the mountains and across the plains and came again to the castle of King Manus.

THE RETURN OF KING MANUS'S HORSES

AGAIN Manus, King of the Western Island, sat in his supper hall. The torches were in their sconces, the candles were lighted on the table, the hearth fire was blazing on the hearth, and his lords once again sat to the right and the left of him. But this time they sat without laughter and without high words.

The harper and the storyteller were at the table too, but they neither made music nor told stories. They had tried, both, that evening, but no one had listened to them. Outside, the iron door of the stable gaped wide, and the grooms and horse-boys and watchers stood idly around or went quarreling among themselves. It was very difficult, as you may imagine, for the harper to play upon his harp when he would hear the King say into his wine cup, "O, Raven, my black horse, where art thou now?" And it was equally difficult for the storyteller to get on with his tale when he would see the King looking at him with unseeing eyes and hear him say, "O, my white and my red horses, what would I not give if I saw you back in my courtyard again?"

So you can imagine the silence that was upon the supper board that once resounded with conversation and storytelling, with music and pledges of the wine cup. "O, Raven, my black horse, where art thou now?" said the King once again; and then, "What would I not give to have my white and my red horse in the courtyard again?" And these were all the words that King Manus could be got to say.

And then, suddenly, a loud neigh was heard outside. Straightway King Manus ran out of the supper hall. The lords, the minstrel, and the storyteller, the stewards, servers, and attendants, ran with him. And when they came as far as the wide door of the castle they ran into the grooms and the horse-boys who were running from the stable. All ran together. And there, in the middle of the courtyard, without a rider upon his back, was Raven, the King's black horse.

They brought him into his stall in the stable, and they combed him and they groomed him. They gave

him the red wheat and the white barley to eat and the
clear spring water to drink. King Manus could hardly
be prevailed upon to leave Raven's stall and come
back into the supper hall. But at length they got him
back into his seat, and then the supper board resounded with pledges of the wine cup as the King and
his lords drank to each other merrily.

Again there was neighing in the courtyard, this
time a double neighing. Straightway the King ran
out, and all who were near ran with him. They ran
into the grooms and the horse-boys who were running
from the stable. There in the courtyard were the
white horse and the red horse. They were not un-
mounted, however, for Eean and Bird-of-Gold were
upon them.

This time King Manus grew into such glee that he
swore by the open hand of his father that he would
make a duke of every lord who was with him that
night. There were great rejoicings. Some tossed their
torches so high that they frightened the owls out of
the cornices on the castle. The grooms brought the
white horse and the red horse into their stalls in the
stable, and they fed them with red wheat and white
barley and gave them the clear spring water to drink.

Then they went to carry Eean and Bird-of-Gold
into the supper hall. They were not to be found for a

while, for Anluan, Eean's father, had led them away. He was seen to weep over Eean, and to take the hands of Bird-of-Gold and kiss her while he called her daughter. And to Anluan King Manus gave the privilege of bringing them to the supper board.

The King put Eean into the storyteller's seat, but he had Bird-of-Gold sit beside him on his left hand. The feast began all over again and went on from egg to apple. And when wine had been drunk King Manus called upon Eean to tell the story of his journey to Merlin's Island and the full tale of how he had defeated Zabulun the Enchanter.

When all was told the King gave presents to Eean and Bird-of-Gold and he swore that for a year and a day he would have them live with him in his castle. "And," said he, "this girl, Bird-of-Gold, has been very loving and faithful to you as you have been to her, and for a further benefit to you I shall have the old blind sage come down from his attic in the castle and marry you here and now." Eean and Bird-of-Gold took each other's hands as he said this, and the old blind sage was brought down from his attic chamber, and he married Bird-of-Gold and Eean by the rays of the rising sun.

For a year and a day they lived in King Manus's royal castle. Now Eean had learned so much of the

arts and crafts and mysteries that belong to an Enchanter that he was able to do great works for the
King. Castles he built that gave security, and bridges
that brought people together, and mills that ground
for the people abundance of corn. He had become so
strong and so sure of himself since his encounter with
Zabulun that all he set out to perform he did well.
And his wife, Bird-of-Gold, loved him so much that
her thought never went back to the country she had
come from. Always, they say, she kept a flock of
white ducks; perhaps they reminded her of the thousand ducks that was the fortune she brought into
Babylon.

But the storyteller must not forget to tell you about
the question that Eean asked Merlin the Enchanter on
King Manus's behalf. It was about a game of chess
that King Manus had been playing with his brother-
in-law, King Connal, for half their lifetimes without
either having victory in sight. Moreover, they had
inherited the game from their fathers, and it was now
being played for fifty years. Merlin told Eean what
the moves should be, and the day after he came to the
castle, Eean took the chess board and showed them to
the King. With that instruction he played. The game
of chess was finished three days afterward, and great
fame and honor came to King Manus.

ABOUT THE AUTHOR

Born in 1881 in Ireland's County Longford, Padraic Colum grew up surrounded by the traditional culture of Ireland. When still a young man, he joined the National Theatre movement in Dublin, and his play *Broken Seal* was produced when the author was only twenty-one years old. He was one of the founders of the *Irish Review* in 1911 and was its editor until 1913. Since 1914, Mr. Colum has made his home in the United States. This country is richer for having acquired, even by adoption, an author so full of whimsy and the feeling of Ireland.

Padraic Colum typifies the best in the Irish renaissance. The mixture of gaiety and shadow that is so much a part of the Irish heart is his, and with that subtle twist of English speech that only the Irish give it, he has written poetry, dramatic legends, fantasies, and stories for children that have won him a high and lasting place in English literature.